BEAUTIFUL SHAME #2

RANDALL & HUDSON

MA INNES

1

HUDSON

IT WAS a rough bar in an even worse part of town, and I couldn't figure out what the little twink was doing working there. Well, I had an idea, but nothing that made sense. I had to be wrong. It'd been a few weeks, maybe longer, since I'd stopped in, but I knew I would have remembered him if I'd seen him before.

BJ's was technically named after the original owner, but it was also a really big clue about what someone might find going on in the back room most nights. It'd been a gay bar as long as anyone could remember, and most of the customers had come out in a time where you were either tougher than the bullies or you stayed deep in the closet. Most of them looked like they'd just gotten released from the state pen, even though I knew they all had regular jobs and were actually upstanding citizens.

But when they walked into the bar, most of the trappings of civilization fell away. So I wasn't sure what the hell Jake had been thinking when he'd hired the little twink. Pushing away from the wall where I'd been watching for the last few minutes, I headed toward the bar. I found an open spot in the corner and waited for Jake to wander over.

Customer service wasn't his thing.

He finally finished up with a big bear of a guy with tattoos down his arms and started heading my way, stopping long enough to grab me a glass of whatever he had on tap. The words were out before I could stop myself. "When did you hire the twink?"

Jake laughed and gave me a knowing look. "Few months ago. He's good for business. But only works a few shifts a month, unfortunately. He's like honey to those dirty old barflies. He just reels them in, then walks away."

"He looks too innocent to be working in a place like this."

"Hey, my bar's clean and the men behave themselves pretty good. They might be doing their best to make him blush, but they keep their hands off. Besides, he likes the attention. The raunchier, the better." Jake glanced over at the boy where he was trying to clear off a table, but every time he bent over to grab the glasses at the far end of the booth, catcalls and whistles rang out.

The tight skinny jeans and slim-fitting black shirt that rode up showing a strip of his back did nothing to hide the full ass that arched out as he reached for the dirty glasses. I was all the way across the room, and I could easily see how he gnawed at his lower lip and blushed when the men called out.

Jake was right, the men didn't lay a hand on him, even though he was a tempting bit of sin.

"Why only a few shifts a month?" How had I not seen him before? Had it really been that long since I'd been in?

I owned a moving and trucking business that had one of its main offices down the street. Between putting in extra hours there because of some staffing issues and my regular job at the uptown location, I'd been working crazy hours lately, but it hadn't been that much, had it?

Glancing over at Jake, I saw him shrug. "I offered him

more, but he just stammers and says that his other job keeps him busy."

"Other job?"

"No idea. I just know he calls himself Rand and only will agree to about four shifts a month. I first hired him to work a few hours here and there to give Andy more time off. Now it's so busy when he comes in, I could use two servers." Jake gave me a long look. "Maybe he'll give you some incentive to come in more often too."

I just snorted and ignored him, but didn't even try to pull my gaze away from the blushing twink. There was just something about him. A contradiction. He'd flirt and then ease off. He'd blush at a terrible dirty joke, but he never backed away completely. It was almost like he was encouraging them, but there was a layer of embarrassment that was pulling at the men.

It pulled at me too.

"Hell, maybe having you around will make him come in more." Jake laughed at the confused look I sent him. "Present company aside, because I'm *very* taken, you're probably the only decent guy in here. Compared to these roughnecks, you look like one of those models in the underwear ads. If he blushes and gets turned on by these bozos, I can't imagine what you're going to do to him."

"You're insane."

"I'm right. You just wait and see." Jake smirked and walked off toward the other end of the bar.

A couple of shifts a month wouldn't make a difference in anybody's budget, so there was no way he was working there for the money. He was hot enough, with that ass and that fiery blush, that he could have made a fortune at any of the upscale clubs in the better parts of the city.

I wasn't up for the high-maintenance guys that swarmed in those bars, but the little twink would have had them eating out of his hand. There were a few tattooed bears that were sexy in a rugged way, but unless the little guy was head over heels for one of the regulars, there wasn't enough eye candy to use that as an excuse.

Why was he at BJ's?

Why wasn't he putting up more of a fuss about the comments they were making?

And why in the hell was he that turned on?

The tight jeans and the sheer size of his cock didn't leave anything to the imagination. At first, I thought I was wrong. But when he walked over near the bar, returning the tray of dirty glasses and bottles, his erection was obvious.

It snaked down his pant leg, the thick cock nearly perfectly outlined. I couldn't help but look. We were probably about the same length, though I was maybe a little thicker, but with his thin frame and short stature it looked out of proportion, making you think it was huge. There was no way the guys would have missed it.

Hell, there was no way anyone could miss it.

It was no wonder they followed him with their eyes and did their best to tease the little twink. He loved it. Was it the raunchy humor and the dirty words? Was it being watched… lusted after? Did he love to tease the guys…show them what they couldn't have?

In other bars, the twink might have run into problems flirting and flashing that monster, then refusing to play. But Jake was right, he ran a good bar. The guys were rough around the edges, but I couldn't see any of them actually scaring the boy.

Making no attempt to disguise my interest, I watched as he dashed around the room, bringing drinks and cleaning up messes the men deliberately made. Finding reasons to get the boy to bend over seemed to be the game of the night; the dart board on the wall sat empty and even the lone pool table in the back was deserted.

Not that I could blame them; he was more interesting than anything else in the place.

After cleaning up the same booth three times, because the men kept shoving empty glasses to the back of the table just to get the boy to bend over again, he finally came back over to the bar. "I need three more beers, they said whatever's on tap, and a whiskey sour."

I was expecting a lighter voice, something more feminine, but it came out rich and sexy. It was easy to imagine how he'd sound turned on and begging. He was a mass of contradictions and it only made him more appealing.

Jake took a couple of minutes longer than it should have to get the drinks ready, but it gave me a chance to see the boy relax against the bar. At first, he was just focused on the mirror behind the long shelves of liquors, watching as the men leered and stared. It didn't take long for his gaze to wander around the room while he fidgeted and waited.

He nodded and smiled at a few of the regulars who were too laid-back to take part in the teasing, but it was obvious when he got around to me. I couldn't have been looking at him any differently than the rest of the men, but his blush flared back to life and his big eyes flicked down to his tray before peeking back up at me.

I couldn't decide if he was that good of a flirt or if it wasn't an act at all.

Either way, it didn't matter.

It'd been a long time since I'd done the bar scene looking to pick someone up, and even longer since I'd explored the darker parts of the city, playing in a different kind of scene altogether. I gave in to a one-night stand occasionally, but that wasn't what I wanted. Finding a guy who wanted something a little rougher but still serious was hard. When you added in the rest of the shit and baggage, it was almost impossible.

Jake had to clear his throat several times before the twink looked over at him. "They like looking at that ass of yours, but not for long if you don't give them their drinks."

He blushed an even deeper red and gave me a cautious glance before he mumbled an apology to Jake and picked up the tray. As he stepped back from the counter, his long cock was still clearly outlined. When he caught me watching him, he sucked in his lower lip and lowered the tray so it almost hid his arousal.

Curious.

Did he not want me to get the wrong idea, or was he actually trying to hide how turned on the teasing made him? It was hard to tell. Moving around the men and mismatched tables, he handed out the drinks, blushing and all the while giving me sidelong glances that were sending out mixed messages.

"You've certainly caught his eye."

I snorted and shook my head. "I'm new to him."

"He's not here enough to know most of the guys. They're all new. You're just different."

"Different?"

"Hot and hungry. You look at him like you want to eat him up." The soft voice that came from behind me had me turning on the stool.

"I thought he was here to give you some time off?" Andrew, or Andy to his husband Jake, hopped up on the stool beside me and grinned.

"How can I stay away? I'd miss the floor show."

One eyebrow went up, and I gave him a curious look. "What floor show? It's not a strip club."

Andrew laughed. "He keeps his clothes on, but those guys couldn't be any more worked up if he were naked and shaking it. They're probably more turned on because he's fully clothed, and god, that blush. I'd kill to look that innocent and erotic at the same time."

"Hey, my man is sexy, and don't you forget it." Jake gave him a long look, and I knew he was going to spend the night reminding his husband just how hot he was.

Andrew snorted. "I'm hot—but nothing like that." He glanced over at the corner where the twink was bent over, trying to get a napkin that one of the guys had *accidentally* dropped on the floor.

With anyone else, the move would have looked contrived and borderline ridiculous. The twink made it work...like the coy looks and embarrassed arousal were just who he was. When he caught me watching, he turned slightly. So I couldn't see how erect he was?

"Now that's a new development." Andrew's voice pulled me away from the view.

"What?"

"They drop that napkin two or three times a night. He always gives them one of those blushing smiles, but he's never tried to hide before. That must be for your benefit." Andrew studied me for a long moment. "Maybe he's finally found someone here he's actually interested in."

"So he hasn't dated any of the guys or given anyone a hint that he'd be okay with more than just the teasing?" Hiding my interest would have been ridiculous. I wasn't going to play those kinds of games with anyone.

"Oh, no, the first week a few guys tried, and he shot them all down. He likes the teasing, but he doesn't encourage them beyond that," Jake broke in, frowning as someone called him down to the other end of the counter. "I guess I should say he *usually* doesn't encourage anyone."

I wasn't sure if he was trying to keep me away or if he had no idea what he desired. If he wanted me to back off, the hesitant glances and nervous looks weren't the way to go. They were only making me more curious...more intrigued.

"If he's trying to encourage me, he's clearly not sure about it."

Andrew sighed like the whole thing was one of those overly sweet romance movies. Considering the fact that my thoughts were decidedly more NC-17, I wasn't sure he understood the situation. "Those shy looks and the way he's trying to hide how turned on he is...it's so cute."

"Why?"

"Why what?"

"Why's he trying to hide?"

Andrew looked at me like I was crazy. "How many guys do you know who'd want to share that kind of a kink or whatever it is before they've even had a chance to flirt?"

"My last two serious relationships started with a contract. I'm the wrong person to ask a question like that to." I turned back to see my little twink cleaning off another booth while everyone watched, drooling. "Is he an exhibitionist?"

Andrew laughed, but it came out more as a giggle. "Maybe? Jake thinks it's the teasing that gets him off."

Something certainly was getting him off because his cock was still rock hard and I could see his nipples, puckered and erect through the T-shirt. "That shirt is like two sizes smaller than the rest of you wear."

"Yup." Andrew grinned wickedly. "After the first week, I told him it shrunk in the dryer and gave him a tighter one. He just blushed and tried to hide that monster before he went in the back to change clothes."

That put wicked images in my mind. "You're terrible."

"You'd have done something worse."

"I'd have made the shirt thinner. Like those shirts from that other vendor. The cheap, almost see-through ones that Jake hated." Jake had put his foot down about his husband wearing something that sheer, but they would have looked incredible on the boy.

"Oh, I forgot about those. He'd love it. I think they're still in a box somewhere. That packrat of mine doesn't get rid of anything." Andrew licked his lips and watched as the server started walking back toward the bar.

"You're making Jake crazy."

"Yup." Andrew gave me a side glance and winked. "On days Rand works, I get hammered as soon as Jake gets home. Most of the time we don't even make it to the bedroom."

"He remembers you're a bottom, right?" I'd known the two men too long to pull any punches or beat around the bush.

"If anything could tempt me to top, it's that ass right there." Andrew and I both watched as the boy bent over to pick up another dropped napkin.

The cautious look the boy gave me as he was bent over, flashing that ass to the men behind him, had my cock stirring. He might be worried what I'd think, but there was definite interest there. "I'm going to be the only one topping that perfection."

"I want my fifty bucks!" Andrew grinned and hollered over to Jake.

Jake turned from the customer he'd been talking to, looking indignant and frustrated. "You cheated."

"Did not." Andrew smirked and ran his thumb over his fingers in a clear *money* gesture. "You just lost."

"You were betting on me?" It didn't surprise me at all.

I got another look like I was stupid. "Of course."

"Why did Jake think I wouldn't be interested?" That was the part I couldn't figure out.

"Oh, we both knew you'd want him. Jake just thought it would take another night before you made a move."

That had me laughing. "And you didn't?"

"Hell, no, I remembered how long it's been since you've

talked about anyone. Your right hand has to be exhausted." He smirked as Jake started to stalk over, the thirsty customer forgotten.

"Thanks."

"Welcome."

"You cheated. You said something." Jake growled the words out, convinced he was swindled.

"I'm just smarter. You can pay me when we get home." Andrew turned his hot gaze to his husband. "Or I might be willing to discuss a deal. If you make it worth my while."

"No sex in the bar, you two."

Jake shook his head and barked out a laugh. "No sex in the front of the bar, you mean."

Giving Jake a look, I pointed to the boy who was inching his way up to the counter, trying to get Jake's attention. "Come on up, Boy. I don't bite."

"Unless that's what a cute little twink is into." Andrew's smart mouth couldn't resist, and seeing how it made the little thing blush, I knew he hadn't tried very hard to hold back.

"That goes without being said. Got to give a boy what he needs." I ran my gaze up the twink's tight body, making a long stop on his hard cock before I brought my eyes up to lock with his. "Every boy or sub needs something different."

2

RANDALL

I WAS EITHER GOING to die of embarrassment or a heart attack. Maybe both.

"I'm Hudson."

It took me a minute for my brain to catch up with what the extended arm meant. The sex god wanted to shake my hand? "Um, hi."

I'd already set my tray down, so I awkwardly stuck out my hand, letting his fingers wrap around mine. It was like lightning went straight to my dick. The strong, hot grip and the desire flashing through his eyes made my knees weak.

I probably looked like a moron, but all I could do was stare at the sinful expression that was aimed at me. It was like a porn star walked out of a movie and was waiting there for me. I'd kept telling myself that up close he'd look sexy but not so drop-dead gorgeous.

I couldn't have been more wrong.

He was like a GQ model in one of those expensive suits, but there were hints of something rougher. Something just a little naughty...dirty. Or maybe I was projecting. I'd seen similar expressions before. Sexy guys who gave the impression of walking on the wild side, but who, in reality, never did more than spank a guy during sex.

I was tired of being the freak—the guy who looked so innocent and sweet that no one could ever get past what I fantasized about. He was interested, but did he understand? I hadn't been able to stop responding earlier. The looks...the teasing...it was all too much.

Maybe it would have been different if I'd been afraid or worried, but Jake had pulled me aside the first night and explained that the customers would flirt and probably drive me crazy until I set boundaries, but then they'd respect them.

Damn, he hadn't been kidding.

They had the worst pickup lines and the dirtiest leers, but they'd never touched me. And after I turned down offers for dates and blowjobs, they didn't ask again. The way I'd blush and stammer when they made comments about my ass and bending me over only encouraged them.

I just hadn't realized how much I'd like it.

When I'd first worked up the courage to answer the ad online, I'd thought I could handle the temptation. I'd work a few shifts, and the rest would be my dirty little secret. One I'd only let out in the safety of my room—in the privacy of a dark, locked room.

But there'd been no way to hide it.

The first comment from one of the regulars about me being so tiny one good fuck would break me had me so hard there'd been no way to hide it. And when the uniforms got tighter, the teasing only got worse.

Hudson didn't look like the rest of the customers, though.

He wasn't the type to make a dirty joke at my expense and walk away. He'd never drop a napkin on the floor to watch me bend over...he'd just bend me over himself.

"Randy. Randy."

It took me a moment to hear Jake. I couldn't take my eyes

off Hudson, but I managed to answer the frustrated voice. "Yes?"

"They're waiting for their beer. And if you keep them waiting, they're going to drop more than just that napkin. Your ass is fine, but I'm not cleaning up anything crazy." Jake's tone was teasing, and I could hear Andrew giggle, but I couldn't help blushing.

My gaze dropped to the floor automatically. I didn't want to see what Hudson thought.

Before I could grab the tray, with my insane cock trying to decide if we were actually upset or still turned on, a finger lifted my chin until I was staring my GQ god right in the eyes again. "Follow instructions, Angel. And they can drop anything they want as long as they look but *don't* touch."

"They don't touch." That probably wasn't the best response, but it was all I could think of. I should have told him not to touch me either...or pulled away...or something besides look at him like a lovesick puppy — a *dirty* lovesick puppy.

"Good. You go have fun teasing the guys then, Angel." Hudson's gaze dropped to my clearly hard dick and back up to my face. "It looks like you've been having a good time already, though."

My face was probably the same neon red color as the open sign that flashed in the window, but I couldn't help it. I also couldn't help the way my cock liked the attention we were getting. It was just naughty enough...just humiliating enough that it pushed me so close to the edge I almost exploded right there.

I nodded stupidly and started tripping over my tongue when Jake cleared his throat and looked down at the tray on the counter. "Drinks. Yes. I'm sorry."

"Good boy, Angel." The words sent shivers down my spine, and I desperately tried to hold in the moan that wanted to escape.

I just kept nodding—because how was I supposed to respond to that—and picked up the tray. As I walked away, I heard Jake question Hudson, "Angel?"

Andrew sighed. "With those looks, you have to ask?"

Hudson's reply had the moan breaking free. "A dirty, fallen one...but still an angel."

His low chuckle followed me across the room. As I handed out drinks and tried to appear reasonably functional, the customers quickly figured out the easiest way to fluster me was to mention Hudson.

I got to hear how he was watching me...what he was doing...and my personal favorite...what they thought he was going to do to me.

I was completely insane—but Hudson didn't seem to mind. And that was just weird.

There was no censure in his eyes, and no judgment in his expression...he just watched me flirt and blush, his gaze getting hotter as the evening went on. By the time I'd made two more trips up to the bar, I'd been able to talk to him more, and he was starting to look like he was going to pounce on me at any moment.

Did I want him to?

Probably.

I'd never been pounced on. I'd never been much of anything. When your insides didn't match your outsides, guys got confused. Guys who looked sweet and blushed got treated with kid gloves...not leather gloves that could spank and punish them.

And there was *no* way to explain that to a nice guy who wanted to take me to the symphony or to the art museum.

The art museum wasn't going to get him into my pants when what I really wanted was to be manhandled and taken. I'd only tried explaining that to one date before he'd accused me of wanting to be raped and left me at the restaurant, telling me he wasn't going to date a crazy guy, no matter how hot I was.

After that, I just went out on the boring dates and kept the real me to myself.

I could still hear the venom in his voice when I thought back to that night. Maybe I wasn't completely normal, but I wasn't as bad as he'd made me out to be.

"You're a million miles away."

I should have sensed Hudson coming up behind me at the bar, but I was a bit too lost in my own head. His arms came up to rest on the counter, almost wrapping me in his arms, but he was careful not to touch me. I jumped and inadvertently fell into his arms, rubbing my ass over his surprisingly hard cock before he could help me stand up.

"Oh!"

I could hear his chuckle, but I was too embarrassed and too trapped to turn around. Besides, the fantasy of having him pinning me against the counter and touch me was too good to resist. I wouldn't let just anyone touch me. I knew how to say no—but something about him made me desperate to say yes.

Maybe it was the look in his eyes.

Maybe it was the way he watched me.

Maybe—

"And there you go again getting lost. Am I that boring?"

"God, no!" And that came out a little more honestly than I'd planned.

"So you're thinking about me?" Heat dripped from his voice. I could feel him getting closer, not touching yet, but I knew all it would take was one little move, and I'd be pressed up against him.

Lie?

Truth?

"Yes." It was all too perfect to lie. I wasn't sure if this was a single chance to live out my fantasy, or something more, but either way, I was going to grab onto it.

"You were so distracted that you missed a napkin and a spoon on the floor. Go pick them up for me, Angel. I can't have you leaving a mess lying around, can I?" He stepped back and moved one hand from the counter, pointing to the odd objects on the floor.

Eager, wicked expressions watched the new turn of events, and I could almost see some of them holding their breaths, waiting to see what would happen. It took my brain a moment to catch up. "Pick them up?"

"Yes, go be a good boy and show me how you do it." The way he said the deceptively innocent words had my cock jerking in my pants and pushing against the already tight material. "Go on and be a good boy, you don't want to have to be punished here in front of everyone, do you?"

"I...I..." The answer was supposed to be no, I knew that.

I just couldn't manage to say it.

He let out a wicked chuckle, obviously understanding my dilemma, and leaned in even closer so his breath danced over my neck. "I'm going to remember that, Angel. Now say, 'Yes, Sir,' and go pick them up."

"Yes, Sir." Just saying it made my knees weak, and a little moan escaped. There was no hiding how much I wanted him... wanted what he would do to me...

Even if I'd managed to hold in the desperate, needy sound, the ridiculously tight pants would have shown him just how turned on I was. If I wasn't careful, I was going to end up with a wet spot on the front. And just imagining *that* made my dick throb against the rough fabric. Wearing something under my pants wasn't an option, they were too tight, and hiding my cock wasn't really the point.

I was so good all the time; it was my only form of rebellion...of getting what I needed...

Walking toward the napkin and spoon on the floor felt like the longest steps of my life. It wasn't unexpectedly discovering that the men would make lewd comments if I bent over...this was deliberate. He would know what it meant. He would understand I was giving him permission to do more than just gawk and turn me on.

Wouldn't he?

I thought just going to work where they would know what I liked was the hardest thing I'd ever done, but it was nothing compared to that moment, that one instance of second-guessing and indecision. Taking a deep breath, I stopped fighting what I wanted.

I bent over, making sure to keep my legs straight and stick out my ass, picking up the napkin and spoon that were lying there so innocently. There was almost complete silence as I straightened and turned around to bring the items over to Hudson. No whistles. No comments about how sexy my ass was, or how it should be sculpted. That was Jacob; he was some kind of artist and a little bit weird.

They were the biggest bunch of nosy drama queens.

Now was the hardest part. I wanted Hudson, and everyone else, to understand that I was changing the rules for him, and him alone. Jake made a comment one time about everyone leaving Andrew alone because he'd claimed him, and the men understood that. Well, they needed to understand that Hudson was the only one who could push the boundaries I'd set up.

If he wanted to.

God, please let him want to.

"Good boy."

The way he said it sent shivers down my spine. "Thank you...Sir?"

It came out more as a question than statement, and I glanced over at him to see him smiling, giving me a little nod.

He was back to sitting on his stool, legs spread, highlighting just how aroused he was.

I turned him on.

Well, something I'd done turned him on. What was it, though?

Obeying him?

Watching me bend over?

Calling him "Sir?"

Knowing everyone was looking at me?

I knew I shouldn't question whatever naughty deity had dropped him in my lap, but it was all too good to be true.

"That's right, Angel. Have you ever had a master?" He said it like it wasn't the craziest thing anyone had ever asked me.

What weird rabbit hole had I fallen down where that was a real question? "No, Sir."

And how did I get more of the insanity? "But I…I…"

I couldn't get the words out. I wasn't even sure what to say or how to explain any of it. I'd never had anyone to talk to about the weird things that ran through my head. No one in my real life would understand.

I'd thought working here, on the few nights I could sneak out, would be all that I would get. It felt like a huge chunk of what I'd needed for so long, but I was starting to see it had only been the smallest taste, and Hudson was offering me more.

Master.

Hudson watched as I tried to sort through everything that was happening. Before I could say anything, Andrew grabbed my arm and started dragging me away. "I'll help you clean up the table again."

Table?

Laughter sparkled in Hudson's eyes as he glanced over toward the back of the room again. "It seems like you missed a table, naughty boy."

Andrew was giggling as he practically ran us toward the

booth at the back of the room. It was one of the longest tables, and nearly every man in the room had put at least one bottle or glass toward the back of it just to watch me bend over.

Andrew never had to clean the table, and he wasn't even working, so I wasn't sure what he was doing. "What—"

Andrew jumped over my question, charging right in. "Okay, so Hudson's only going to give us a minute before he starts distracting you again, and the rest of the motley crew around here aren't going to be any better, so I have to hurry."

Andrew started holding up fingers like he was remembering a grocery list. "Here's what you need to know. He's a nice guy. Functional, with a job and everything. Shipping and trucking. He's a total Dom. The whole getting turned on while people are watching you thing isn't going to put him off. Make sure you set up a safeword so he knows when you're actually saying no to something. Oh, and don't do anything stupid that gets you both arrested when that cop comes in."

He blinked at me and started chewing on a nail, clearly trying to think. "That's probably about it. Let me know if you have any questions. Call the bar or something."

No. Calling wouldn't be a good idea.

"I will if I need to." I couldn't picture anything I'd actually be able to ask him or tell him about, but it seemed to make him feel better, so I didn't feel bad about the lie.

"Good. He's hot and super kinky, but not into, like, bed hopping or anything, so you don't have to worry about him sleeping with other people. He hasn't had anyone serious in his life for ages now." Andrew sighed dramatically. "You're going to have so much fun."

His eyes started to sparkle with mischief. "Maybe if I gush enough to Jake about how hot you two are going to be together, he'll go all caveman on me tonight." Then a wicked grin danced across his face. "Lean over and grab the drinks so I can ogle your ass again. That makes Jake so jealous, one of these days, he's just going to bend me over a table and go for it right here."

I knew my face had to look almost purple with embarrassment, because there was no way red would describe my level of surprise. With everyone watching, including Hudson, it wasn't like I wanted to resist, though. And the idea that Andrew had been watching me too was…interesting.

"God, you're hot when you go all turned on and red. I need to learn how to blush." He sighed and leaned against the booth, watching me just stand there. "Clean up, you know they're waiting."

And I was dying.

But it was *so* tempting.

I bent over. People didn't seem to understand you could be a virgin and a slut, but I was both, and I just couldn't help it. It was like lightning went down my spine and straight to my dick every time I knew they were watching.

Being the center of attention in my *real* life would have been a nightmare, but in a place like BJ's, the wicked part of me was set free. I was probably going to hell. But knowing they wanted me, even when they knew I wouldn't have sex with any of them, just made it impossible to do anything rational.

At least, that was my excuse when I pressed my cock against the table and ground it against the smooth wood as I reached for the glasses. Andrew let out a low moan and a little whistle, which only made the men go even wilder—which only made my cock harder and my brain work less.

It was a vicious, dirty cycle.

Sliding against the table as I cleaned it up, I silently cursed the jeans for not having enough friction. I'd never come when I was working, but knowing Hudson was watching made it so insanely tempting. By the time I had all the dirty glasses and bottles on the tray, I was nearly panting and so hard the seam of my pants was pressing into my cock painfully.

The delicious shame just fed the flames, and I had to reach down and adjust my dick before I could pick up the tray. I blamed *that* on a lack of oxygen and blood to my brain. The customers playfully leered and called out ways I could fix the problem.

Glancing across the room, I saw Hudson moving one finger in a come-here motion. I couldn't decide if his dark expression meant he was turned on even more or mad. Maybe both? Picking up the tray, I weaved my way through the room. If I put a little more sway in my walk, I wasn't going to admit it.

Setting the tray on the bar, I crossed the short distance to stand in front of the man I was quickly becoming addicted to. His gaze was fiery as I stepped between his splayed legs, trying to get as close as I could to him without touching. His muscles were straining at the white dress shirt, and even with his sleeves rolled up and his collar open, he gave off the impression of pure power.

Did I believe in love at first sight?

No.

Did I believe in obsession at first sight?

Absolutely.

"You were close to coming, weren't you, Angel?" There was censure in his voice, but not for teasing everyone or for just generally being a slut.

"Yes, Sir." I didn't try to hide my response. Everyone was so quiet the slightest drag of a chair echoed. There was no way and no reason to hide. I wanted them to hear.

His gaze scanned down my body, clearly enjoying what he was seeing. "I want that cock to stay hard. You're going to leave it on display, Angel."

I couldn't have been any closer to coming than I was right at that moment. "It's hard."

Difficult. I should have said difficult. He just smirked. "I know. And it's going to stay that way."

Blushing what had to be the color of an overripe tomato, I nodded. "Yes, Sir."

"When do you get off?"

It took me a minute to figure out the question, because my first thoughts hadn't had anything to do with time. Looking at the clock behind the bar, I was surprised to see how much of my shift had already passed. "Ten minutes."

"Good." One of his fingers started to trace around my hand where it was resting on the smooth wooden counter. Less than an inch separated his fingers from mine, but he didn't touch me. I could almost feel the heat from his body. It sent need flooding through me in waves.

I wanted that touch more than anything else I'd ever had dangled in front of me.

Every present and trip, every reward and gift couldn't compare to the desire I felt right then. "Go finish your shift, Angel."

I just blinked at him. Shift? It took me several long seconds before the words connected in my mind. "Yes. I have to… and…" I looked around the room, a little lost, lust clearly fogging my brain. "Yes, Sir."

Stepping away from him was one of the hardest things I'd ever done. Everything in me just wanted to throw myself at him, but that wasn't how it would work. Whatever *it* was, he was going to take the lead. I could see it in every movement he made. He'd give me everything I wanted, I could see that too, but it would be at his pace and under his control.

So. Fuckin'. Hot.

3

HUDSON

"THAT WAS SO erotic I could come right here." Andrew looked like he'd melted into the counter, hanging over it like a wet dishrag. "Like the best porn ever. Baby, you have to let me work nights with Randy. I don't want those nights off anymore. I gotta be here to watch this."

Jake's response came out more as a growl than real words. "Hell, no."

"But, baby, did you see them?" Andrew pulled himself up off the counter and slinked over to Jake. It wasn't as good as the sexy walk that seemed to come naturally to the boy, but it was hot enough for Jake to forget why he was frustrated, because he just watched as Andrew wiggled and flirted. "They just make me wa—"

Jake evidently thought the only way to shut up his husband was by keeping his mouth otherwise occupied. As they kissed, and Jake did his best to devour his man, I went back to watching my wicked angel. He was so damned innocent and sexy it was almost criminal.

"How old is he?" Giving myself hell for not asking before, I looked away from him long enough to toss my napkin at the still-kissing lovers. "Age."

They broke apart enough for Jake to toss me a grin. "Legal. Mid-twenties."

The boy's innocent blush and unquenched need made him seem younger, but I was glad to know I was pushing the limit but not robbing the cradle. I was only in my mid-thirties, so it wasn't that bad. He might be young, but my angel seemed to know what he wanted—just not how to get it.

I was going to help him out with that.

As he moved around the room, the men clearly understood his shift was nearly done, so that meant the floor show was almost over. They finished up the last of their drinks and threw tips down on the tables.

They called out goodbyes to Jake and Andrew, and even tame "When you comin' in again?" and "See ya next time, Randy," and one simple nod with "Hudson's a lucky man," which I thought was funny. The boy just blushed at all the attention and stammered out cute responses as the men grinned.

When there were just a handful of stragglers who'd hang around until the bar actually closed, the boy went up to Jake and started making sure he had everything finalized with the bills that had been paid. His eyes kept flickering over to me, and the way he was swaying against the bar, I knew he was trying to get himself off.

I wasn't sure if it was something he realized he was doing or if it was subconscious, but either way, it was distracting as hell. With where he was standing, most of his body was hidden, but my brain could easily fill in the blanks. I'd studied him enough that picturing his sexy body wasn't a problem.

There was some clear hesitation in his eyes when he was done for the night. He stammered out some last-minute information for Jake, then stepped away from the bar. "I need to get changed before I go."

I got several long looks, but I wasn't sure I knew what they meant. He obviously needed some reassurance that I wasn't just going to disappear on him. I wasn't sure how much of the innocence was just his natural response, or how much of it meant he really was just that innocent, but he couldn't have had that many men in his life.

He was just too open and honest with his reactions.

As he walked toward the back where I knew there was a small employee bathroom that doubled as a locker room, I did my best to dig out my patience from where it was buried. It was hard to find. Everything in me wanted to follow him and —

"You know he's back there jacking off, right?" Andrew's voice startled me, and it took me a second to follow what he was saying.

"He's what?"

Andrew just grinned and shrugged. "He goes back hard and comes out soft. You do the math. And don't either one of you give me shit for noticing. If he wanted to hide it, he should wear baggier pants."

Oh, no. That wasn't the plan.

"I'll be back." Making no move to hide where I was going, I started heading back to the locker room, with Jake and Andrew calling out opposing instructions.

"Make sure he's okay with you being in there. Don't rush the boy."

"Go for it. He doesn't want you to hold back." Andrew was clearly not worried about me scaring the twink.

I'd been going to the bar for years, so even with the maze of small rooms and locked doors, I knew where my boy was. I gave one firm knock and tried the handle. Locked. "Angel?"

He didn't ask for explanations or what I was doing there. He just opened the door and peeked around it curiously, one bare shoulder showing he'd already started getting undressed. "I'm not done yet."

That was the point.

"I know. Let me in." I reached up and cupped his face, trying not to smile as he leaned into my touch and blinked up at me. "We can talk right here if you want to, but we're going to have a talk about you playing with your cock in there before you finish changing."

His face blushed so deep I could feel the heat radiating from it with my hand, but his eyes got that lust-filled look that made me want to do wicked things to him. Things he'd love. It only took seconds for him to make the decision, and he stepped back, opening the door wider.

I ran my thumb over the bridge of his nose, then moved my hand away. He was too much temptation. We needed space until we had at least a short talk. I had to know what he was thinking first. "Good boy."

He gave a low moan and licked his lips. God, he was responsive.

I could only picture what he'd be like in bed or pressed up against the wall. As I walked into the room and headed over to a chair that was shoved in the corner, he glanced back and closed the door.

The internal debate was obvious, and I wasn't going to influence it. Closed or open, locked or unlocked, whatever he needed to feel safe was fine. Considering he'd only known me a few hours, the caution was a good idea.

He finally reached out and locked the door before turning to walk to me. His shirt was gone and the button on his jeans was undone, but his cock was still hard, and I got the feeling he'd quickly stuffed it back in his pants. I'd probably caught him just starting to play with it.

"What did I say about that cock, Angel?"

He took a shaky breath, and his eyes got wide. I would have thought he was frightened or nervous, except for the way his cock jerked. His fingers went to his pants and absentmindedly started rubbing his jeans. Not quite touching his dick, but so close I knew that was what he wanted to do.

"Not to come…to leave it on display." The words came out low, and I could hear the need in his voice.

"Andrew said you'd come in here and jack off after your shift. Is that correct, Angel?" I knew the idea that they knew what he was doing would only rocket his arousal higher.

I didn't know everything that sent the boy flying, but I was starting to get a clue. Embarrassment, and probably shame, seemed to be rushing through him, but his still-hard cock and lust-filled expression let me know just how much he liked the feelings.

He just blinked at me, and I could see thoughts and fantasies dancing through his head. "Answer me, Angel. You don't want to be punished, do you? Are you being naughty?"

Oh yeah, the idea of being punished only got him closer to his orgasm. He let out a ragged moan, then shook his head. I knew there had to be a huge part of his brain pushing to see what would happen if he was punished. He finally got the words out, though, stuttering and blushing, fighting the need and embarrassment. "I'm sorry. Yes…I…I was going to…to play with myself."

His brain seemed to finally kick in gear, because the words started coming out clearer. "You didn't say I couldn't come." The boy blinked up at me, his wide eyes filled with need. "I left…it on display."

"The rules are going to change if you're going to be my boy. I realize we don't know each other very well yet, but I'm going to be honest and tell you that I'm drawn to you, and that I want to see you again."

"Like date?" There was the slightest pause, and I could see him steeling up his resolve. "Not just fool around?"

"Yes, and be your Dom." I was probably going too fast, but I couldn't force myself to slow down and back off. "I'm not going to rush you into something you're not ready for, but there would be different rules if you want to be my boy. Do you want to be mine, Angel?"

He blinked down at me and looked lost, like it was completely overwhelming, and he didn't think it was real. I didn't fight the need to gather him into my arms. "Come here."

Reaching out, I took his hand and started to pull him closer. He glanced down at our clasped fingers. It didn't seem to help him snap out of what I thought was shock, but he followed my lead. When I pulled him down to straddle my lap, he moved almost automatically. Even knowing he was on display for me and open to my touch didn't seem to break him out of it.

"What's going through that head, Angel?"

He gave me a hesitant look, then moved his gaze back down to our hands where they rested on one of his legs. I was doing my best to ignore the fact that I could feel his cock against my hand. He was slightly softer than he'd been a few minutes ago, but even confused, he was still responding.

When he finally spoke, it was low and quiet. "Even after everything that happened out in the bar? I mean, I know that's not what guys want when they're serious with someone, but I…" The words trailed off and he peeked up at me, caution and worry evident in every movement.

"Of course." It was quickly becoming obvious that he'd never dated anyone in the lifestyle or even remotely kinky before. "I had fun, and I liked seeing you enjoying yourself. You were having a good time, weren't you?"

I got a hesitant nod, but his tense body was starting to relax. "Most guys…it's like that lecture my dad used to give me before he found out I was gay…the 'there are girls you marry and girls you don't' routine. I know you're not saying you want to get that serious, but still…"

"And you were thinking you fell into the latter category because you liked being watched and teased?" God, what a horribly old-fashioned and misogynistic thing to say to a kid. "Every serious relationship I've had was with someone who knew what they wanted sexually and weren't afraid to go after it." Some were more knowledgeable than others, and what they wanted varied, but they all had the same internal drive to figure out what they needed.

"Just because you're an exhibitionist, and probably into some humiliation play, doesn't mean there is anything wrong with you or that someone won't want to date you. I can feel you up in the bar at work while everyone watches, and then go to dinner with you after. It's just different parts of the same relationship; neither one is bad or dirty."

His eyes widened when I talked about feeling him up in the bar, but it didn't seem to help his confidence. He didn't call me out and say he didn't believe me, but the denial was clear on his face. No amount of talking was going to convince him. His parents had evidently done a number on his sexuality, and it would take time to *show* him I was telling the truth.

"How about this…what are you doing Friday?" I was probably going to have to work late again tomorrow, but by the weekend, things should be back on track or heads were going to roll.

"You want to go out?" Again the words were cautious. "A date?"

"Yes, dinner, and then we'll do something fun. Do you have to work?"

He shook his head when I asked about the schedule, but his expression was still troubled. "Angel, I'm not sure there's any kink or desire you could have that would chase me away. You're not married, right? Not seeing anyone seriously? Not hiding from the mob? Witness protection?"

He grinned, and his soft fingers started caressing mine, no longer holding on for dear life. "No. Not married. No mob bosses after me, either."

"So there's nothing to stop us." Seeing his smile and feeling his body relax, I took that as a hint I could turn the conversation around to something more fun again. I moved my hand so my fingers could start trailing lightly over his cock.

The reaction was immediate.

Another low moan escaped, and his dick jerked and started to thicken. "We were talking about you playing with this pretty cock, weren't we?"

When I lightly scraped a nail over the head of his dick, he gasped and shook, but he managed to respond in a breathy voice that was so hot I wanted to push him even more to see what other beautiful sounds I could get out of him. "Yes."

"That's my good boy. You want to be mine, don't you?" Teasing his cock wasn't helping his higher brain functions, but he seemed to do better and react more honestly when he couldn't think, so I didn't feel bad.

"Yes...please..." His body gave a desperate thrust, and he tried to push his length harder against my fingers. "Please, I've been so hard...all night..."

The sentences were broken and needy, but he was so damned responsive it was amazing. "Does my wicked angel want to come? Your cock's so hard. I bet you want to touch it so bad, don't you?"

"Please...Sir...please let me..."

"That's right. If you're mine, I get to control that sexy dick of yours. You're going to have to beg nicely to play with it and come. I'm going to tease you and have so much fun with it. You want to give me control of that hard cock, don't you, Angel?" I whispered the words into his ear, making low circles over the head of his erection with my fingers. It wasn't enough to get him off, but it was enough to completely fry his brain.

"You want all the men who were watching you tonight to know you belong to me. Don't you want to fantasize about me touching you when you're bent over that table? To know that I might do it because your body belongs to me?" I ran my nails over the sensitive head of his dick, and he just about came. His body shuddered, and his back arched with the strain. "Good little slut. You don't have permission to come yet."

I paused long enough to make sure I had his attention. "Are you going to be mine…be my wicked, dirty angel?"

His eyes fluttered closed, and his free hand dropped down to grab my arm. When he gave me a firm nod, I smiled but shook my head. "That's not enough, Angel. Open your eyes and look at me."

He forced his eyes open, but they weren't completely focused, and I knew he was starting to get lost in the sensations running through him. If I could get his brain turned off and the worries to quiet, I knew he'd sink into subspace beautifully. "Good boy."

I gave up the pretense of just holding his hand and released his fingers so I could run mine up and down his hard length. "Who does this cock belong to?"

His breath hitched and a ragged moan came out. Giving it a harder squeeze, I pushed him even further. "Tell me, Angel. Who does this dick belong to?"

He was almost panting when he forced the words out. "You. It belongs to you."

"That's right. You're mine, aren't you?"

His response was desperate and needy. "Yes."

"Then you have to ask permission to touch it. Here, or at home, you have to get permission. When you're at work, before you come back here and tug on that hard dick you've been teasing everyone with, you have to come find me and ask nicely or call me." It was a common rule in relationships that had domination and submission as part of it, but I knew with the way my angel liked to be teased and shown off, I could take it even further. "Do you understand?"

"Yes, Sir. Yes." He was nodding frantically, his hips jerking with the strain to stay still under my caress. He was a natural submissive who wanted to be touched, displayed, and probably used.

He was perfect.

It didn't take him long to understand what he had to do next if he wanted to come. "Please, can I...will you...please, can I come?"

The words were almost frantic, and his body was so tight it felt like he could shatter into a million pieces. Running my fingers along his dick, I gave him the words he was desperate for. "Yes, Angel, you're going to get to come. Let me see that pretty cock you've been teasing everyone with all night."

His hands were shaking too much to get the zipper down, and even as he tugged, he realized that straddling my lap made the pants too tight to push down. He scrambled to get off my lap and would have fallen if I hadn't been holding on to him.

A low chuckle rolled out of me, and with some guys it might have upset them, but it just fueled the fire inside my wicked angel. The groan of relief as he finally freed his cock and shoved his pants down was throaty and deep. He quickly shoved off his jeans and shoes and threw himself back into my lap.

His skin was smooth and free of hair. It was obvious that my boy liked to shave, because even his treasure trail was gone and the area around his cock was bare. He didn't seem to be shy or hesitant, so I didn't worry about where to touch as his naked body started wiggling on mine.

One hand landed on his ass to keep him from falling over, and I brought the other up to cup his balls and tease around his erection. "My beautiful boy."

He writhed and whimpered as I teased his cock. "So sexy and smooth. Nothing to hide this pretty dick or your body. You're beautiful, and I can't wait to run my tongue over all these sculpted muscles." He was lean and would never be a bodybuilder, but his body was sculpted with tight muscles that begged to be touched and caressed. He'd look amazing dressed up in nothing but a tiny little jock and paraded around.

Low moans and little whines escaped as I ran my hands over his chest and balls but left his cock alone. When I let one finger slide back and flick over his tight puckered hole, he gasped and words started tumbling out. "Please. Sir. Yes. More. Please."

It wasn't sentences, but it was beautiful.

"Show me how you play with your cock. I want to see you touch yourself. But remember, you don't get to come until I give you permission." The words came out rough, but he didn't mind. Lust dripped from every pore, and even the way he blushed let me know how turned on he was by the order.

His hand moved slowly, but I knew he wanted it, because by the time he wrapped his fingers around his hard cock, he was shaking with desire. A low moan ripped out of him and his hand started flying over his dick, racing for his orgasm.

"Slow down, Angel. I'm not going to let you come that fast." I caressed the sensitive skin around his clenched opening and kneaded one ass cheek. He slowed his hand, but it was a barely controlled jerking motion that I knew he couldn't maintain.

"That's right." I tapped one finger on his hole and roughly fondled his balls, making him whimper again. Fuck. It was the most incredible sound. "If you want to come, you have to be a good little slut and obey your master."

He exploded.

I don't know if it was being called a slut or me referring to myself as his master, but something about the words pushed him over the edge. He arched back and screamed out his need Ropes of cum hit his chest and hand as he tugged on his cock, milking every drop of pleasure and cum from his body.

I gave his ass one swat which only made him louder, and the desire that ran through him more violent. When he finally sagged against me, with little aftershocks making him jerk, I moved my hand from his balls and brought it up to his face.

"You were a naughty boy. Did you have permission to come?" I didn't make any attempt to hide how aroused I was. Even I could hear the need that dripped from the words.

His head came up, and he looked at me with a foggy, sated expression. "I couldn't help it...you said...and it just...and I..."

"You're going to have to be punished, Angel." I shook my head like I was sad, but I knew my face held a wicked grin, because he started to squirm again. "I'm going to have to figure out a good way for you to remember who controls that sexy cock."

"I'm sorry?" He was obviously torn between feeling bad that he'd disobeyed and the excitement of being punished. The unknown would keep him on edge and constantly ready. "I'll be good next time. I promise."

"I know you'll try, but I'm still going to have to punish you." I squeezed down on his ass, letting my fingers inch closer to his opening, just so I could watch the pleasure flare in his eyes again. "Do you understand that, Angel? You need to remember who has the control."

"You do. You." He whimpered again and tried to push his ass harder against my hand. "Please?"

"No more tonight." I gave him another pop, loving the way he arched and gasped. "You were naughty."

"But—" He sat back. His lower lip poked out in a sexy pout, giving me the sweetest look.

"No, Angel. When you show me you can be good, I'll let you come again."

He inched toward me and tilted his head. "After my punishment?"

"Yes." I leaned close and pressed a tender kiss to his lips, swallowing the little gasp that escaped. Pulling back, I smiled before settling into the chair. "I'm going to enjoy punishing you, Angel."

He couldn't seem to decide what to say, but his blush spoke

volumes. My needy little slut was excited too. "Let's get you dressed. They're going to want to see I left you in one piece after that scream."

He groaned and blushed, but his quick peek at the door, and the way he licked his lips, said he wasn't *that* upset. When he tried to stand, I gripped his hips and shook my head. "That's not how naughty, dirty boys clean up their mess."

I took his cum-covered hand and brought it up to his lips. "Show me how you should clean it up, Angel."

His gaze bounced back and forth between his hand and my face. Checking to make sure it was what I really wanted, maybe? I was betting his internal debate over what was "bad" and "naughty" was raging.

Finally, he took that step, and his tongue flicked out, licking some of the cum from his hand before darting back in his mouth and looking at me, hesitant and unsure. The desperate need for someone to understand him was so clear it made something inside me hurt.

"My sexy boy. Show me again. You've got cum all over, Angel."

That sweet blush was back. His tongue peeked out and swept over his palm before he sucked his pointer finger in his mouth, deep throating it like a porn star, all while having that angelically innocent expression on his face.

I wasn't sure why we were clicking so fast, but it felt right. It was like one of those movie moments where viewers could see the entire plot turning in a new direction in just one scene. It wasn't something that the audience was expecting, but it made everything even better.

But no matter how long we lasted or what happened, I was going to do my best to show him that words like *naughty* and *wicked* and *dirty* and even *slut* didn't have to mean negative things. I wanted to show him that knowing what he wanted and what he needed out of a relationship didn't make him a terrible person. I also wanted to show him that he could take control of his sexuality and his desires by giving that control to someone else.

My boy was made to submit, and I was going to show him how.

4

RANDALL

"HE CALLED ME ANGEL...HIS dirty, fallen angel."

Even whispering the words into my dark dorm room sent swirls of crazy things going through my head...and my stomach. He seemed to get me. And he didn't think I was some kind of insane whore with a mental disorder.

It probably meant he was a stalker, and I'd end up dead somewhere—but it would be worth it.

Hell, just imagining the look on my parents' faces as they were interviewed about my grisly death would be worth it too. Okay, so he probably wasn't a psycho. Andrew and Jake wouldn't have been pushing us together so hard if they thought he was crazy.

Before the cab had even dropped me back off at the dorms, my phone had nearly exploded with the volume of texts I'd gotten from Andrew. He'd been demanding to know what had happened in the back room and if I was going to see Hudson again. I also got hell for "sneaking" out the door before he could talk to me in person.

I hadn't needed to sneak out. He'd been too busy mauling his husband to notice anything that was going on around him.

After Hudson had watched me get cleaned up, he'd cuddled me and even helped to get my clothes on.

I'd gotten some weird looks as I stuffed my jeans into my backpack and put on my regular clothes. But walking around town with my dick outlined like that didn't seem like a reasonable idea, so I thought I might have misunderstood his expression. As we'd walked through the bar, he'd asked if I needed a ride home or a walk to the bus, but I'd already arranged for a taxi.

There hadn't been much of a chance to actually talk, but he'd given me a stern look and said he was going to fix that. Then he'd cracked a terrible joke about not being interested in me just for the way my ass looked in my jeans. I'd laughed and willingly added his number to my phone.

He'd said he would call, but I wasn't sure if that meant soon, or just eventually. I hadn't really had enough second dates to know what the rules were. I also wasn't sure if the previous night counted as a date. He'd had a drink, and we'd technically met at a bar, and I'd had one hell of a goodnight kiss. So maybe it *was* a date.

I really wished I had someone to ask.

You'd think after six years of college I'd have found someone to talk to about stuff like that, but there wasn't anyone. Looking around my room, I wasn't sure how it had happened. I knew people. There were other students I could call to study and hang out with, but no one who I shared anything personal with.

And *everything* that had happened with Hudson was personal.

The first couple of years at college, I'd been so focused on my classes that finding real friends hadn't been important. I'd double majored in history and English, finishing both in just over three years, so most of my *free* time had been spent studying. When I'd added in family commitments, there wasn't much left over for me, let alone anyone else.

It had been painfully clear that I wasn't destined to follow in my father's footsteps and take over his company, so they'd decided that academics would be a good path for me. My mother had said having a professor in the family would look good, and I hadn't cared enough to argue with them.

And if staying in school kept me off their radar, then I was going to stay in college as long as possible. Multiple master's programs and planning for a doctorate I didn't really want was keeping me pretty busy and their friends impressed, so I wasn't going to rock the boat until I had a backup plan.

That was almost impossible, though, because they were firmly against me working. Every time I agreed to work hours at BJ's, I kept expecting them to jump out and start asking me what I was doing. "Mom, I know you said you wanted me to focus on my studies, but I decided I wanted to work a few shifts at a gay bar in a part of town you wouldn't even take an armored car through."

Yeah, that would work out great.

"Did you say something, man?" My roommates voice called out from the living room.

Shit.

"No!"

There weren't that many people living on campus getting their master's—because who in their right mind would want to do that—but there were just enough people to fill the top floor of one of the dorms. Luckily, it was suites with small private rooms and a shared living room and kitchen, but it was still living on campus with strangers and very little privacy.

I'd tried to talk my parents into getting an apartment, but I'd gotten shut down so many times I'd given up. Once I picked the doctorate program I was going to apply for, I thought I might get another chance. Their friends would think it was weird if their son the *almost-doctor* was living in the dorms.

The last time I'd brought it up, my mother had talked about me moving home. I wasn't going to do anything to put myself in that position ever again, so I was going to have to be careful. Just the handful of times a year I had to show up for parties at the house or some function or another were bad enough.

Living there full-time would require anxiety meds or something.

Glancing over at the clock, I was glad to see it wasn't that late. Sometimes after I'd been at the bar, I was so worked up that it took hours to fall asleep. But last night, I'd gotten home and crashed. Hard. No staring at the ceiling. No marathon jerking off sessions. No fear about what might happen or what they thought. Last night had been perfect.

So, of course, I was waiting for the other shoe to drop.

It would eventually. I wasn't going to let myself believe that Hudson would do anything wrong. But sooner or later, I was going to say something insane, or he'd figure out I didn't belong in that part of town and move on to someone who fit in. There was also the possibility that my parents would figure out everything, and then all hell would break loose.

But I was going to enjoy it while it lasted.

Sexy, built men who were gay, open-minded about kinks, and not psycho weren't exactly a dime a dozen, so I was going to do my best to push back my worries and live in the moment. Now I just had to figure out the best way to do that…and the rules…my mother always said there were rules of etiquette for everything, you just had to figure them out.

Well, none of the manners I'd ever been taught included situations like last night.

Hudson had talked about domination and submission and had wanted to be called Sir, but I wasn't sure exactly what that meant. I wasn't a moron, or so isolated I hadn't found porn, but

I wasn't sure what parts of that were real and what parts were just for movies and in people's imagination.

Did guys really kneel?

Did they really call someone Master?

Did they actually give their Masters complete control?

Well, that one might be real. I thought I might have given control of my cock to Hudson. *Maybe*. He'd seemed so serious when he'd said it, and the way he'd looked at me when I'd agreed had been insane…off-the-charts hot.

Was there a good way to text him and ask if that part was real or just for fun?

Real people and couples did role-playing stuff. That was fairly common, if daytime television shows were correct. Was last night just something like that? A fun game at the bar but not a rule he was actually serious about? The rational part of my brain said it had been entertaining in the moment, but that was it. There was another piece, though, a quiet but persistent one, that said I was being delusional.

It was convinced he was serious.

I wanted him to be serious.

I desperately wanted it. Maybe that was why it seemed so unreal. I'd never met anyone that took control like that or talked about sex the way he had. Did that mean I was really supposed to text him or call him when I wanted to come? That wasn't…it had to be…

My head was confused, but my cock clearly liked the idea, because the half-hard morning wood I'd woken up with was starting to turn into a full-on erection that I didn't want to ignore. I looked down the bed, where my cock was covered, and then over to my phone on the nightstand.

Could I actually do it?

Was I supposed to?

After a few more minutes of the weird internal debate, I still hadn't come to any conclusions. The obvious answer seemed to be to text him and ask if he was serious, but if he wasn't, that would be embarrassing. And would probably be sharing too much about what I desired.

But if he was serious, he'd want to know what I fantasized about…right?

I was saved from myself by a notification from my phone. I was expecting some kind of message about a study group for this weekend or even a random doctor's appointment reminder…anything but Hudson.

His name flashed across the phone as I swiped my finger over the screen to open it.

Hope I'm not bugging you at work. Jake said you had another job.

Well, it was starting out normally enough. And he had said that he was going to talk to me soon. This was soon. If he actually wanted to date, hiding school seemed like a waste of time, so I texted him back.

Not bugging me. I'm a student. Master's program…most of my classes are later in the afternoon and in the evening. I'm in my room not doing much right now.

His reply came back immediately. Wasn't he supposed to be at his office?

Makes sense why you aren't there much…evening hours and classes don't mix.

Kind of…and there was the whole panicked about getting caught part.

Yes, but I like work.

His reply made me laugh.

I liked watching you work.

That had been obvious. And surprising.

I noticed.

I wasn't sure what he was going to say next, but his response was…interesting.

I also noticed that you liked being noticed.

My brain didn't know how to respond to that. *Yes* seemed

too stark and too...dirty to admit. He seemed to understand that because I got several messages in a row.

There's nothing wrong with wanting to be watched.

Or teased

Or talked dirty to

I wasn't sure I believed him, but disagreeing with him sounded rude.

It's hard...I'll try?

And that looked pathetic even in a text message. At least he hadn't been able to hear the confused whiny voice that was in my head.

The phone started to ring.

Shit.

Not answering wasn't an option—because he kind of already knew I had the damn thing in my hand. Taking a deep breath, I tried not to sound as panicked and confused as I felt. "Hello?"

His low chuckle made my cock jerk. "You sound nervous, Angel."

Well, that hadn't worked. Might as well be honest. "Yes. I've never...Well, this is..." I sighed and took a deep breath. "And now I sound like a moron."

Hudson laughed. The tone was so rich I could almost see the smile on his face. "You sound like a confused guy after his first time submitting. That's normal. And it's the reason I called. I wanted to make sure you were okay and see where your head was."

That was...sweet. But I still didn't know what to say.

Or how to ask the million-dollar question.

"My head's...*weird*?"

That low laugh came over the phone again. "Weird, huh? I guess that makes sense. Is your dick confused or does it know what it wants?"

I could feel my face heating up, and a little noise escaped,

43

half-whine and half-moan. "Um…it's *not* confused."

That damn laugh came through the phone again and my cock jerked. It was so tempting to reach down and wrap my fingers around it, but that…that would be wrong. Right? His voice dropped lower, and the deep sound vibrated through me. "Does your cock like what happened last night? Did it like getting teased and shown off, then touched?"

"Yes."

"Tell me more, Angel. I know you're probably blushing and hard. Aren't you?"

"Yes." He wanted more? Hiding and denying everything seemed like the most logical option, but a bigger part of me wanted to please him. No matter how embarrassing it was…or maybe because it was so embarrassing. "I…you watched me… and then you…and you touched me…and made me strip…and the rules…"

I kept tripping over the words that were rattling around in my head. Nothing would come out right, and full sentences seemed to be beyond me. It was easier when he was right there, and I could see his face. When I could be confident that he meant it, and he was turned on too.

"You like being watched…do you know how sexy that was?" Rustling sounds came over the phone, and I wasn't sure what he was doing, but my mind was filling in all kinds of naughty things.

"It was?" He'd gotten hard, and he'd been turned on, but…

"It was, Angel. I got to see you wiggling that ass and bending over for everyone. And you were so good when you did what you were told and obeyed me." Desire was thick in his voice, and I squeezed my legs together, trying to get enough friction to come without actually touching myself.

"Did you like obeying me, Angel?" The low, wicked words did crazy things to my stomach. "Did doing what you were told turn you on even more?"

It was hard to force the words out, but eventually, I managed. "Yes. I liked...liked knowing what you wanted, and that you were turned on...too."

"You are perfect, Angel. I bet you want to touch that pretty cock. Don't you? Is it hard?" I could hear the desire in his voice, but he seemed to think the question was perfectly normal, while it sent my insides whirling again.

"Yes...can I...I have to...I mean...asking and..." I took a breath and started again, refusing to keep going if I sounded like an idiot. "Yes, I'm hard." Ha! I did it. "And I'm supposed to ask about...playing with myself, right?"

Nothing like that had *ever* come out of my mouth before.

"Very good. Yes, you need to ask before you play with your cock. You gave me control over it. Right?"

"Yes." The word was a little squeaky, but I got it out.

"Then, when you're hard, and you want to touch yourself, you need to text me or call. Sometimes I'll say yes, but sometimes, I'm going to say no. Like last night when you were working. I wanted that hard dick on display, and that meant you didn't get to come right away. It was worth the wait, though, wasn't it?" He was making me crazy. I'd never met anyone like him.

"God, yes...it was so hot...perfect."

"I'm glad, Angel. I'm going to show you all kinds of things you're going to love. I still haven't forgotten that you need to be punished for coming without permission. Since it was the first time you disobeyed, I'm going to give you a choice about your punishment."

What?

"A choice?"

"Yes. Since you're hard and needy right now, you can choose not to come until we have our date this weekend, or you can come now, but you need to know I'm going to punish you at work next time you have a shift. Which one are you going to pick?" He said it so logically, like we were picking pizza toppings or something.

"Um…"

It wasn't like picking pepperoni or sausage.

"Come now or wait?"

It wasn't that simple.

He would punish me at work.

"What would…what would you do at work?" The idea of being punished in front of everyone *should* have scared the hell out of me.

That low chuckle came over the phone again. "Nothing you'll hate. But you will remember it, my wicked angel."

My eyes closed, and it took everything in me not to grab my cock. "I don't know what to do."

His voice took on a sweeter note that was just as sexy. He honestly seemed to understand how difficult it was, how taking that step was almost impossible. "Do you want me to pick? Do you want me to decide your punishment?"

"Yes." Then I wouldn't have to feel guilty…he was choosing. I'd given Hudson that power, so it wasn't up to me.

"All right, Angel. I want you to say something for me first."

"What?" Something in his voice made me want to squirm. It was going to be naughty.

"Say, 'Master, please decide my punishment.' I want to hear you say it, Angel." His voice was rough, and desire flowed through the phone down into me.

My dick was straining in my briefs, and they were sticky with precum. I'd never been this turned on unless I was at the bar or fantasizing about wicked things. It was the most insane, naughty, incredible situation that had ever happened to me.

I had to keep reminding myself that it wasn't a dream. That made it even harder, but I wasn't going to pretend that I didn't want it. I wanted it more than anything. "Master, please decide my punishment."

Master.

Hottest. Thing. Ever.

"Good boy. I'm picking the one I want more. Do you understand that? This is the one that's going to please me the most. I'm going to like punishing you, Angel. I'm not going to hide that. I know you're going to do your best to be a good sub for me, but when you disobey or come without permission, I'm going to love punishing you."

Fuck.

"Yes." It came out anxious and desperate.

"I'm going to discipline you at the bar. Everyone will know you've been bad. But that means you get to come now. You want to touch your cock. I can hear it in your voice." Frantic sounds came out of me, and he gave a low hum of pleasure. "My needy boy. Reach down and touch your dick."

"Now?"

He wanted me to do it now? Like phone sex?

"Have you ever touched yourself while someone listened, Angel?"

"No!"

"Oh, sweet boy." He sounded like I'd just handed him the keys to Versailles and said it was his for the taking.

"I haven't…I haven't done much." My hand snaked down under the covers and my clothes and wrapped around my cock. I just couldn't hold myself back anymore. If I was quiet, he wouldn't be able to tell what I was doing.

"Angel, I'd love to be your first. I'd love to be your first *everything*."

The pleasure short-circuited my brain. That was my only excuse. "You would be my first everything. You were my first kiss."

His moan shot pleasure right through me. "God, Angel. You make me crazy. I can't wait to see you again."

I tried to drag out the pleasure. I tried to slow down and

make it last, but it was impossible. I was racing after it as fast as I could. I clamped my lips together, but he heard something because his voice got heated and wicked again. "You're playing with your cock. Are you going slow, or are you going fast?"

A little whine came out, but something in me pushed me to answer. "Fast. I have to…faster…"

"Because you want to come. You're my wicked angel. Are you on the bed?"

Thinking was hard and talking was even worse. "Yes… under…in bed…"

"Push the covers down. I know you're hiding that pretty cock of yours, but I want it out." He only gave me a second before he kept giving me orders. "I can hear how hard you're breathing. Let go of your dick, Angel, and push down the covers. I won't tell you again."

The tone of his words had me shaking. That strong, demanding voice knew exactly what it wanted. My obedience. "Yes, Master. I'll be good."

I didn't want him to change his mind. I needed to come.

Shoving the sheet and comforter down, I moaned as the cool air of the room hit my cock. Hudson just knew without my saying anything else. "Good boy. Grab lotion or something, I don't want you to come too soon."

I whimpered. "Please…but I need—"

Hudson broke in, his words firm and commanding. "You need to obey your master, Angel."

"Yes, Master." Damn. That was the hottest thing ever. "I'm sorry."

Apologizing probably wasn't supposed to be so erotic.

I reached over and grabbed some lotion I kept in the nightstand. I didn't use it very often. I liked the feel of my dry hand on my cock. Rough and almost painful. It made me feel naughty, which only made me come faster. The lotion made a dirty sound as it came out, and I didn't even take the time to warm it up before I was grabbing at my cock again.

The cool feel made me gasp, but the friction of my hand against my cock made it heat up quickly. "You like it rough, don't you, Angel? You want it to hurt just a little."

Pathetic, needy sounds spilled out of my mouth, and they just made me grip my dick harder. "Yes. I have to...I need to...more..."

"You want more? You want me to let you come?"

Was that what was holding me back?

I wasn't sure. All I knew was that I was so close I could feel my orgasm rolling through me, but I couldn't get there. I needed to come. "Yes. Please!"

"Keep playing with your dick, but I want you to tug on your balls. Remember, I don't want you to come yet."

I released the sheet I'd had a death grip on and reached down to grab my balls. Rolling them between my fingers, I teased at them for a moment before giving them a tug. Lightning shot through me, and I gasped out, "Please!"

"That's a good boy. Again. Let me hear how wonderful it feels."

The mix of pain and pleasure had me whimpering and crying out. I needed to come. He had to let me. "I need...I can't wait...Master, please."

He must have heard the desperation in my voice, because he finally took pity on me. "Pinch the head, Angel. Show me how you like the pleasure. Make it hurt like I would. I'd give you what you need."

A strangled sound came out as I took the head of my dick between my fingers and obeyed his instructions. Electricity shot through me and everything went white.

"Come."

There was nothing left in me but to obey my master.

It was the hardest, most violent orgasm I'd ever had. It

rolled through me and just kept going as I tugged on my cock, soaking up the wonderful sensations that came from touching the oversensitive, tender skin.

When it was finally over, and I just lay there panting and jerking as the last sparks of pleasure shot up my spine, I picked up the phone from where it had fallen on the bed and reached for a tissue to clean up the mess. I probably should have been mortified about what had happened, but hearing his voice was the only thing on my mind. "I'm sorry. I dropped the phone."

Hudson laughed, rich and deep. "So fuckin' sexy. I'm going to take you out tomorrow night. When are you done with classes?"

Tossing the mess toward the trash can, I leaned back on my pillow and pulled the sheet up over me again, not even bothering to pull up my pants. That required too much work.

"Eight. It's not a late night." My brain was fuzzy, and everything was going soft. I just wanted to close my eyes and sleep more. The sheets felt silky against my skin and I felt like I'd run a marathon. "A real date?"

His voice was warm and soothing, making me sink deeper into the wonderful sensations still flooding through me. "Yes, Angel. A real date."

"That's wonderful." I yawned and snuggled down into my bed, closing my eyes. "And you won't tell me I'm a whore who wants to be raped."

There was the slightest pause, but my brain almost didn't catch it. "No, I'd never say that. You're my angel, and I know what you need."

"You know everything…so perfect…"

There was another low laugh. "I don't know your real name. Randy, isn't it?"

I smiled, and another yawn came out. "Randy is a nickname. Sounds better than Randall, like I fit in there."

"I like Randall. Maybe Randy when you're my slut. That's a better nickname for when you're being a dirty boy."

"Angel. Already have a nickname from you."

"Who says I only get one?"

I wasn't sure. The question didn't make sense. "Rules somewhere."

"Go back to sleep, Angel. I'll text you about the plans later."

"Yes, Sir. Sleep." That was an order that would be easy to obey.

"My wicked angel." His voice was far away, and thinking was too hard.

"Yours."

He said something else before he disconnected the call, but my brain didn't catch it. The phone fell back to the bed, and I told myself I'd only sleep another hour or two. Then I'd get up and function. Oblivion was right in front of me when I heard a knock on the door that made me jerk and open one eye.

"You okay in there?"

Shit!

5

HUDSON

"DO we have the second round of interviews set up for the warehouse manager position yet?" Glancing up at my assistant as he walked in the room, I frowned at the look on his face. "No? What happened?"

Wes, a guy in his late thirties that looked more like a butler than a secretary, walked toward the desk shaking his head, not a wrinkle in his impeccable suit or a hint of a five-o'clock shadow. I, on the other hand, looked like I'd been left in the washer too long...wrinkly, kind of sad, and a bit too fuzzy for the office.

"I'm sorry. The delay in calling about the second interviews has made things more difficult. Of the four applicants, two have accepted other positions, one has moved out of state for more opportunities, and one is now a resident of the state penitentiary on charges of bribery and assault with a deadly weapon. However, from what I was told, there are other charges that are going to be brought."

He said it with such a straight face I thought he had to be kidding. "What?"

"Evidently, he was stealing money from his previous

employer. When it was discovered, he tried bribing the admin that uncovered it. That altercation did not go well, hence, the assault charges. A letter opener was mentioned."

"You've got to be kidding."

"No. Unfortunately not. The man's soon-to-be ex-wife was very eager to unload some of her frustrations. I'll have HR repost the job and see if we can get more responses."

"At this point, I think it would be easier to replace me than that damn warehouse position." I was only being slightly dramatic. Albert, the previous manager, had done a great job for almost as long as I'd been alive. But no one had noticed mild Alzheimer's setting in until the office was in such bad shape it was going to take someone months to get it all worked out.

Right now, that lucky person seemed to be me—partly out of necessity and partly out of penance.

The company wasn't that big, and I should have known something was up. I'd just thought he was slowing down, and the delay in getting his reports in was because the new systems were a little hard to learn.

Patty, his wife, kept telling me not to beat myself up because even she hadn't noticed how bad things were getting, but that didn't make me feel any better. Merrick Trucking was an international trucking and moving company, but we took great pride in being a family. As head of that family, it was up to me to notice when people were having problems.

"Yes, it would." Now the twinkle was very clear in Wes's eyes, but the rest of his face was still very somber.

When Albert had first given his notice and talked about retirement, no one had realized anything was wrong. It wasn't until we'd started looking for reports and trying to get things organized so he could train his replacement that we began to understand the scope of the problem. Once I'd realized how much effort it was going to be to get that position ready for a new employee, we'd had to put off hiring someone.

The delay had only been for a few weeks, but it looked like that was going to set us back again. "Are you sure there isn't anyone internally that wants the job?"

He just shook his head. "No, unfortunately, we're a small company without tons of extra employees and sadly, everyone is happy where they are. It's tragic."

"The sarcasm isn't appreciated."

"It is, however, necessary when you ask me the same question every time we discuss the matter." Wes didn't believe in putting up with anything from me. It was a little like I was being groomed and tweaked until I resembled the kind of person he thought a CEO should be.

He'd told me once that I was still a work in progress.

It didn't matter that I'd taken over after my father had stepped down five years ago and had managed to almost double the company revenue, without adding a lot of unnecessary bulk. I'd done a damn good job. Wes, however, was very clear that someone in my position had an image to uphold, and I wasn't trying hard enough.

If he wasn't such a good admin, or secretary when he'd pissed me off, I'd have probably thrown him out the window a long time ago. It wasn't like he'd changed after he'd been hired, either. He'd always been a shit, but he'd done such a good job, I couldn't complain.

"Okay, have HR post it today before they leave. I know they might have to work late, but if we can get it out before the weekend, that might help. And start scheduling interviews with people as soon as you can, don't wait until you have several good candidates."

"Do you want to open the position to people from out of state?" The hesitation was clear in his voice.

I just sighed and leaned back in the chair to rest my head on it. Closing my eyes, I shook my head. "Not yet; let's still focus on finding someone local and open it up at the end of next week if we have to."

The area around the warehouse was starting to improve economically, and I wanted to try to hire someone local first. The position paid really well, and it would give someone a big boost financially. Unfortunately, we were having a hard time finding qualified candidates. With the amount of paperwork and federal regulations that had to be abided by, not just anyone would be able to handle the job.

"I'll let HR know." His voice was too even.

"That's what you already told them, wasn't it? They've already got it posted, don't they?"

Wes cleared his throat. "Yes. It was the most logical option, and one you agreed might become necessary when we discussed the previous applicants."

Little shit.

"Fine." Before I could say anything else, Wes cleared his throat again.

"You said to remind you that you need to leave the office at five today because of a…previous engagement." It was as close to *date* as Wes was willing to say.

He'd made it exceptionally clear when he'd first applied for the position that he would not be my social secretary, and my personal life was my business. He'd left his previous job suddenly and without any kind of recommendation. The only thing he would say was that some people couldn't respect boundaries.

I probably wouldn't have hired him, but there'd been a few times in the interview where he'd seemed wounded and a little war-torn. Whatever had happened was enough for him to put up firm walls that he wasn't going to take down. I'd managed to worm my way around them just by sheer stubbornness, but some things he wasn't willing to budge on.

I'd made it a policy never to ask about his personal life.

However, oversharing about mine was becoming second nature. I didn't tell him everything, just enough to make him nuts. "I have a date with my angel tonight."

"That's nice." It was almost a personal comment. I was touched.

"You *do* care." There was a smirk on my face as I straightened and started to rise. "Is there anything else that can't wait until I come in tomorrow?"

Wes got a pinched expression, and I knew he wasn't pleased about how many hours I'd been working. But between my regular responsibilities and handling most of the warehouse manager duties, there was nothing that could be done about it.

The guys at the warehouse had been helping as much as they could, but they had other responsibilities, and most had families that needed them as well. Hopefully, we'd get someone in there soon, and my life could go back to normal.

"Nothing that can't wait." His voice was smooth and confident. "I'll put detailed notes on your desk before I leave, and I'll make sure everything looks correct with the job posting as well."

"Thank you." Gathering up a few papers and shoving them into my briefcase, it didn't take me long to start shutting down my computer. "I'll go over the contracts for the new southern route this weekend."

"Very well. I'll get that organized next week as soon as I have your notes."

"Thanks." Wagging my finger at him, I frowned. "Don't stay too late."

He'd been almost as bad as me lately. I knew I was going to owe him a hell of a Christmas bonus. He didn't think I noticed, but he'd been doing as much of the daily, monotonous part of my job as he could since I'd started handling the problems at the warehouse. Wes was staying late, and from the time stamps

I'd seen on a few emails, was working remotely from home as well.

As much as I wanted to tell him to stop so he could have a life, I needed the help. There weren't enough hours in the day for me to possibly do everything, and that grated on me. Going down to BJ's the other night had been the earliest I'd been able to get out the door in almost two weeks.

"I'm gone. Email me if anything comes up, but everything should be fine at the warehouse, so I'm not expecting any issues."

"Of course. I still think you should call—"

"Nope. It's my responsibility. He's golfing and getting ready for that big party they throw every fall. My mother even said something about going down to the beach house early this year. I'm not going to bring him in. We've got it handled, and as soon as we get someone in the warehouse manager position, it will all settle down. Who knows, this time next week everything could be fine."

My normally unflappable admin snorted and shook his head. "You're an idiot."

"But I'm the idiot who signs the paychecks, so you have to pretend to support my decisions."

"Since when?"

"New rule." I got a look that said just how many ways he was plotting my torture. Deciding not to push my luck by egging him on even more, I headed out the door.

Getting off early gave me enough time for a desperately needed nap, a shower, and copious amounts of caffeine. I'd arrived early and worked through lunch to make sure everything would be on track for me to leave the office at a reasonable time. So, except for a sandwich Wes had shoved at me around two, I hadn't eaten much. I was starving.

My free time since Thursday had been taken up with texting Randall. He just wasn't Randy to me, although when I was teasing him, Randy was going to work as well. Something about the nickname made him feel younger or less manly or just embarrassed in general, because he'd start tripping over his words, and I could almost see his blush through the phone.

I'd promised myself I wouldn't push things too far on our date. He wasn't comfortable with sharing, but when he got tired or just incredibly turned on, little things slipped out. I'd already guessed he wasn't that experienced, but knowing I was his first kiss had been incredible. However, hearing how poorly some of his dates had treated him, and how conflicted he was about his desires, was disturbing.

As far as kinks went, wanting to be teased and shown off wasn't that bad. Even tossing in the exhibitionism and his pain slut tendencies, he wasn't the most unique guy I'd ever dated. Hell, I'd met more out-there people in line at the grocery store.

I just couldn't see how someone had misunderstood his needs so badly.

He was so sweet and innocent-looking, I could understand how someone would be surprised. But the inside of the package didn't have to match the outside. We learned that as kids. Some adults just seemed to have forgotten that lesson.

My goal for the evening was to show him that I wanted to get to know him, and not just sexually. I wasn't sure where things were going, but I didn't want him to feel like a one-night stand or some kind of kinky booty call where I only talked to him at the bar.

I wasn't going to take things in a completely vanilla direction, because honestly, our time at the bar had been incredible. But I wanted him to understand that I could see him as a man and as a slut. They weren't mutually exclusive, and he needed to accept that.

As I drove over to the university, I had to grin. I'd known he was young, but I hadn't expected him to still be living in the dorms. Finding out he was finishing up his master's degree made me feel a little less like I was robbing the cradle, but it gave new realism to the naughty student and wicked professor role-playing that came to mind as I drove through the campus.

Following the directions he'd given me, I easily found his dorm. As I parked and started heading up to the door, I saw him already waiting outside for me, pacing around nervously. He'd said he was out of the closet, but early evening on a Friday night had the area packed, so I did my best to behave.

It was difficult.

We'd decided on a casual restaurant not too far from the campus, so the dark jeans and button-down shirt he was wearing were sexy and appropriate. I was just missing his tight pants, because the ones he had on didn't fit anywhere near as well as the jeans he'd worn to work.

"Hello, Angel. Did you get everything done you needed to?" Randall hadn't been out of his study group for long, so I wasn't sure if he was actually ready to go or if he needed a few more minutes.

"Yes." I got a smile, and a faint blush tinted his cheeks. My naughty boy was having wicked thoughts, but there were too many people around us for me to call him out on it.

"I'm parked over there." I pointed toward the end of the parking lot. "Are you still okay with me driving?"

Not pushing things too fast sexually was completely different than not pushing him past his comfort zone on safety issues. One rule I was bound to fail at keeping, the other was one I wasn't going to forget. Any relationship that had a lifestyle component needed to be based on trust, first and foremost. I wanted him to know I would take that seriously.

"Yes." He looked down at the ground, then around at the parking lot. "I talked to Andrew the other night, and he made sure to let me know you could be trusted."

"Knowing Andrew, it was more colorful than that." I slipped one hand behind Randall and let it rest on his back. Leading him down the walkway, I tried to take my cues from his body language, but he was sending mixed signals again.

Randall would lean into my arm and brush his shoulder against mine, but then he'd pull back and look around. I'd get a flash of heat from his eyes, but when he realized what he'd done, he seemed to mentally push the need away. And he was holding his body so stiffly I thought he'd break.

I'd hoped we'd finally started to move past some of the doubts, but we seemed to have taken a few steps backward. Tackling some of it head-on was probably the best decision, so I was blunt. At the very least, I would shock him out of his nervousness. "When do you work again? I have a punishment to dish out."

He tripped slightly but caught himself before he fell. Randall coughed, and a blush heated up his face. "I, um…I—I'll be working next week. Saturday night. Late shift again."

It felt like he was doing his best not to ramble and stutter, but the stilted words only made him seem more nervous. I started running my hand up and down his back as we continued to walk. I wanted him to see there was nothing wrong with what he wanted. Hopefully, addressing it head-on and discussing it reasonably would help him see that. "Good. Then I won't have to wait too long to punish you."

Immediately changing things up, I switched topics before he could get over his shock. If I could keep him slightly off-balance, he'd have a harder time censoring what he really wanted to say and respond honestly. "Have you been to the restaurant before? I don't remember if you said how long you've been in the area."

Randall didn't seem to know what to say. It was obvious thoughts about the punishment were running through his head, but the more mundane question seemed to throw him. "I…um…I've been here all my life. I haven't gone there before, though. I…um…don't date much."

That seemed to be an understatement.

A boy as sweet, and clearly smart if the school reputation was any indication, as Randall should have been asked out a dozen times a week. Maybe I was a bit biased, but we weren't in such a conservative area that finding other gay students to date would be hard.

"Well, I plan on remedying that. Their loss is my gain." I brought my hand up and ran my hand over his head and down his back again. "There are lots of restaurants in the area and other places we can explore. It will just depend on our moods."

I dropped my voice and let the desire that was always humming just under the surface whenever I thought about him peek out as I was talking. His body started to relax little by little, and his confidence was slowly returning.

As we reached the car, I took his hand. "I have a rental because my car is in the shop. One of my neighbor's kids backed into mine, and it's taking a while to get fixed."

That was the less bitter way to describe a spoiled eighteen-year-old who was doing sixty in a thirty-five and lost control of his new sports car, crashing into my Mercedes. I was just a *little* upset. It wasn't really about the cost of the repairs or about the brat's driving, although it was reckless.

My car was even old by neighborhood standards. It was just the first car I'd purchased on my own, without any help from my family, and my attachment was very sentimental. It was going to be good as new soon, and I vowed to never park it on the street again.

"That's terrible." Randall seemed to have lost some of his hesitation, because the words came out with more confidence. "Was anyone hurt?"

"No. I'm hoping he learned a lesson about being more careful, but I'm not sure he's that smart. Some people have more luck than brains." Leaning against the small four-door sedan, I pulled Randall into my embrace.

He'd said he wasn't hiding the fact that he was gay, and we were far enough back in the parking lot that we finally had some privacy, so I wasn't going to overthink it. "Unlike some people, who seem to be very smart."

I glanced over toward the school and then back at my shy boy. "I seemed to have hit the relationship lottery…smart, cute, and kinky. And incredibly sexy when he's turned on and needy."

6

RANDALL

"RELATIONSHIP?" He'd said it so casually it almost got lost in his description of me. Cute? Sexy? So, kinky I could get, but the sincerity in his voice when he talked about me took my breath away. I'd never had anyone in my life who didn't think I was at least a little flawed, if not broken. Did he really think of whatever we were doing as a relationship?

"Yes." His arms tightened around me, and he pulled me flush against his hard body. "I know we're still getting to know each other, but you're not a one-night stand for me, and this isn't casual."

A hand came up and started caressing up my neck and around my ear, making me shiver. His voice seemed to drop lower, and I had to fight the urge to press even tighter against him because the possessive way he was holding me and the semi-public location was, embarrassingly enough, pushing my desire even higher.

"Is that alright with you?" His touch, and everything else running through my head, made it difficult to think.

I finally forced out one word. "Yes."

I wasn't under any delusion that he would stay around. I

was too weird and came with too much baggage for most guys to want to take on. Hell, just my family alone would chase them off. But the idea that he wanted something serious and was willing to call it a relationship was special.

His smile widened and then turned wicked. I wasn't sure what had passed through his mind, but it was something naughty because the hand on my back dipped lower and cupped my ass tightly before moving back up. "Do you know what I've been thinking about, Angel?"

I could hear his deep voice in my head, explaining that I was his dirty angel. Just the memory had my cock hardening. It brought back everything else about that night, and I knew what he was thinking. It was the same thing I'd been obsessing over for days.

"My…my punishment?"

"Yes." That wicked hand turned so he could tease my crack with his fingers. It probably looked completely innocent from a distance, but it felt dirty and perfect. "Why are you going to be punished?"

My cock jerked, and I felt precum start to leak out of it. Nothing had ever turned me on faster. I was going to have a wet spot on my jeans if I couldn't get control of myself. But that was the furthest thing from my mind. I wanted to lose control completely, not rein it in. "I—I…"

I took a deep breath and tried to focus on the words. I hadn't stuttered since I was a kid, but as I'd gotten older, I'd realized that when I was really turned on and flustered, it would come back. Hudson didn't seem to mind, and the way he accepted my nervousness just made me feel even more special. "I was naughty."

That devilish grin flared back to life. His whole body seemed to hum with arousal as he watched me. "How were you naughty, Angel?"

It was clear that hearing me talk about it turned him on. It was incredible. He didn't seem to second-guess it, and hiding it clearly wasn't anything he'd considered. I'd never met anyone who was that honest about their desires. There was still a frightened voice in the back of my head that kept telling me to shut up and not show him how much of a freak I was, but something pulled at me, making that impossible. I didn't want to hide from him.

"I came without permission."

Hottest. Sentence. Ever.

One finger caressed the top of my crack, hinting at where he wanted to be touching, and a low moan escaped that I couldn't hold back. Just thinking about what he might do to me was frying my brain.

"That's right, Angel. And what is going to happen because you were a naughty boy?" The husky sound of his voice made me whimper. I desperately wanted to be his naughty boy.

"I'm going to be punished when I'm at work next week." I probably should have been scared about what would happen, or at the very least, worried, but heart-stopping desire was the only thing that rushed through me whenever I thought about it.

"And I'm going to enjoy every moment of it." His sexy voice was deep, and arousal seemed to drip from every word.

He really was going to enjoy it.

The idea was still mind-boggling. Not that something would turn him on. All kinds of crazy things did it for me, but just the fact that he would honestly admit it was impossible to process. "I—I..."

Hell if I knew what I was going to say, but he smiled, and the hand that had been teasing at my ear came up to cup my face. "I'm not going to hide anything from you, Angel. The idea of punishing you and doing wicked things to you makes me so hard I hurt. There's no reason for me to lie about it. You like that it turns me on, don't you? You like the idea that I might spank you, don't you?"

All I could do was nod like an idiot. My higher functions were completely gone. He was going to spank me?

"Stop that, Angel. You don't have permission to come yet." His voice was stern and did amazing things to my body, but when his hands moved to hold my hips, I realized I'd been rubbing my cock against his. "No, I don't want you to be embarrassed. I like knowing I turned you on. You are just going to have to wait before you can come again."

That matter-of-fact way he talked about things made it hard to feel bad. "You're going to…"

The rest of the sentence was lost in my brain, but he seemed to understand what I was trying to ask, because his eyes sparkled with desire and one hand moved around to grab my ass again. "I might. That's one punishment I might use to remind a naughty boy that he has to obey his master."

Fuck.

His heated expression took on a wicked look. "But there are so many ways I can punish my angel. So many things that would help you remember who you belonged to. Who do you belong to, Angel?"

"You."

It was a fantasy come true, and part of me wanted to look around for the proof that it was just a dream, but the hand on my ass and the press of his cock on mine were just too real. He was everything I'd ever wanted. Commanding, honest desire just radiated from him, and he was completely focused on me. It was insane.

"That's right." He leaned in and gave me a tender kiss, his lips pressing against mine for just seconds, but it was enough to send my entire body flying. My second kiss. "You belong to me."

It was incredible. Beautiful and naughty at the same time. Just like him.

"Yes, Master."

Fuck.

I loved saying that. It made everything tingle, and my cock ached to be touched. Hudson just gave me a look like he was picturing me naked and begging and leaned in, kissing my jaw. Third kiss. His voice came out deep. "Your punishments belong to me."

I got another kiss farther back toward my ear. Fourth one. "Your pleasure belongs to me."

All I could do was whimper as he reached my ear. I felt his tongue trace around the outside shell before he tugged on the lobe with his teeth. It was like a shower of sparks went through me. "Your pain belongs to me."

I whimpered again, but he loved it. He chuckled low and squeezed my ass. "That's right, my little pain slut. I've got so many wonderful things to do to you."

His teeth scraped along my neck, not biting but just giving a hint of the pain that he could show me. I made needy little noises and felt his tongue flick out to lick where his teeth had just teased. It was like he knew every secret button to push me even higher.

"My dirty angel is so needy, so sensitive. I should feel terrible for making you wait." He pulled his head back but left his hard cock pressed tightly against mine. "I don't, though. I like knowing you're going to be hard and needy, just waiting to be allowed to come."

God, the stuff he said.

It took a minute for the words to actually penetrate my brain. I didn't get to come?

Hudson laughed and shook his head. "That sexy pout won't work on me."

I wasn't pouting. "But—"

"You want to please me, don't you?"

Stupid trick question in a sexy voice; he was fighting dirty. "Yes, but—"

"I want you erect and aching while we eat. We're going to talk, and I'm going to get to know you, but I'm also going to make sure you stay nice and hard. And with those baggy jeans, I'm going to have to keep making sure that sexy cock of yours doesn't get soft." The look on his face let me know just how hands-on his checking was going to get.

"Now, climb in. I'm starving, and I bet you are too." It took me a second to follow the abrupt change in the conversation, and it made me want to throw myself at him and whine. If we'd been anywhere else but the parking lot, I probably would have.

"Food. Dinner." Yes, I was hungry, but the need for food was greatly outweighed by the need for other things.

Dirty things.

"That's right; I'm going to take my boy out for a date." His hand came back up to cup my face.

Hudson knew some of the crazy things that bounced around in my head, and he still wanted to date me. It was…mind-blowing. He honestly didn't think less of me for it, and it didn't seem to change how he saw me. I'd never thought I could find someone who'd tease me like he had at the bar, but then want to go out with me in public.

Teasing the slut in a dirty bar was one thing, but then completely changing gears to take that same slut out on a real date was another.

"Thank you."

I wasn't sure he understood what I was trying to say, but he gave me a tender smile and kissed my forehead. "Oh, Angel, you never have to thank me for seeing the real you. I think you are damned near perfect."

THE DRIVE TO THE RESTAURANT WAS SURPRISINGLY NORMAL. I wasn't sure what to make of it.

Hudson was just so…nice…and normal. He talked about random stuff he'd heard on the radio and asked easy get-to-know-you kinds of questions, like what movies I had seen and what books I had read lately.

When I said I hadn't found the time to do a lot of pleasure reading lately, he snorted and shook his head like he didn't believe me. "You double majored in English and history and have all kinds of fun, sexy things running through your head. I just can't believe you don't have a pile of those sexy romance novels hidden under your bed or on your phone."

Those didn't count.

"But…but they…I…" I was a moron who couldn't make words.

Hudson smiled like he understood how hard it was and reached over to take my hand. It was surprisingly intimate, even though it was such a simple touch. "But you aren't supposed to talk about those or admit you read them?"

I nodded. It seemed like the safest response, because words and I didn't mix very well when Hudson was around. He squeezed my hand. "Now I really am more of a visual guy than a reader." He wiggled his eyebrows up and down and gave me a wicked grin. "But when things were less hectic at work, I read a few good ones. I'll have to admit, my favorites were the sexy ones where the naughty little sub gets spanked."

My mouth dropped open. Nothing would come out.

Hudson just laughed and let go of my hand long enough to reach up and close my mouth. "Now tell me about something you read."

He wanted words?

I had to tell him about what I read?

Street lights and passing cars lit up Hudson's face and I could see he was serious, curious even. I just wasn't sure how to start. I'd never talked about my books with anyone. Porn, people understood. Me reading erotic romance novels, not so much.

I didn't watch much porn. I understood the appeal for some people, but I liked getting inside people's heads. I liked hearing why they liked something, and most porn wasn't big on talking. I never got to hear why the guy getting spanked liked it. That was the part I really wanted, because that was the part I didn't understand.

The books at least tried to go into their heads and explain what was turning them on. I kept hoping one day it would click and an author would be able to explain me. I'd open a book and see myself on the pages, so I could point to it and have that ah-ha moment. So far, it hadn't happened yet.

I should have just told him I'd read *War and Peace* recently.

His hand squeezed mine and he started caressing me with his fingers. "Was it a romance or just something fun and sexy?"

Okay, I might be able to do it this way. "Both."

He nodded. "So, plot but lots of sex too?"

"Yes." Relief poured through me. Now it felt more like we were doing it together and not just me sharing my crazy with him, praying he wouldn't see how screwed up my head was.

"Was it a big bear of a guy and a little twink?"

"No." I managed to shake my head that time.

"Was it a Daddy Dom and his boy?"

My mouth might have dropped open again.

"What?" He grinned and seemed to enjoy surprising me. "Those can be hot."

"No." It came out a little squeaky, but my cock jerked in my pants. The images running through my head were just too good.

"Hmm, I think someone's read a few of those before."

Lots of those. The tender Dom taking care of his boy was sexy and pulled me in, but it wasn't something I fantasized about in real life, so it was easier to maintain some distance from the story. That didn't mean I was going to admit to people that I'd read stuff like that.

But Hudson wasn't just anyone.

My nod was a bit shakier that time, and my voice came out a little high-pitched. "Sometimes I have."

It wasn't one word, and I'd actually managed to answer the question, so I was proud of myself. I just had to keep repeating over and over in my head that Hudson hadn't made fun of me for anything yet, and he'd honestly seemed to understand.

It was still difficult.

He nodded like it wasn't a big deal and went back to quizzing me on my most recent book. Like the conversation was perfectly normal. "Was it a businessman and his naughty twink secretary?"

"No." But Hudson was getting closer.

He must have sensed that, because as we turned, his face was lit up by headlights, and he had a wicked grin on his face. "A twink businessman and his rugged secretary?"

Now that sounded good.

"Colder."

That just seemed to spur him on, showing his competitive side. "A sexy businessman and a naughty twink client?"

I gave a hesitant nod. That was pretty close. It was a smoking hot financial advisor, and his newest customer was a sassy young guy who'd just inherited millions. Not the most original plot, but at least there was one, and the sex was off-the-charts incredible. So that made up for a lot.

"Was he just a little bit bad or was he a complete brat?"

The excited leer on his face as he parked made me smile. "Brat."

He turned off the car as we sat in the restaurant parking lot and turned toward me, the seat belt straining across his broad chest. "Sexy brats get spanked."

The words were stuck in my throat and came out sounding a little choked. "Yes…lots…"

"Do you know who else gets spanked?"

Damn.

The word popped out before my brain could even process what Hudson had said. I was blaming it on the fact that there wasn't much blood left in my brain. "Who?"

Hudson's eyes were filled with desire and something powerful that made my stomach turn. "Smart, sexy college guys who love bending over and knowing every eye in the room is on them. Sweet boys who need a sexy master to take control of them."

I was wrong when I thought I couldn't get any more turned on.

7

———————

HUDSON

IT'D TAKEN A FEW MINUTES, but Randall's mind seemed to finally be working again. I probably should have felt a little bit remorseful for turning his brain to butter, but he was just too cute and too sexy when he got all nervous and excited.

By the time we'd headed into the restaurant, he'd lost some of the disheveled I'm-so-turned-on-I-can't-think look, but it wasn't until we'd been seated at our booth that his reactions started returning to normal. If we'd been heading into the bar, I would have kept his need flying, but since we were at a more family-friendly restaurant, I had to keep reminding myself to behave.

Behaving wasn't as much fun.

But it would help me get to know him more. "How were your classes this week?"

He blinked at me several times, like the conversation in his head was a lot different from the one we were having out loud and it wasn't quite connecting. As I started browsing over the menu, giving him time to process the question, he finally nodded absently.

Before I could clarify and see if that was actually his answer, he started to talk. "They were good. The lectures aren't that difficult to follow. The real work comes when we have papers to write. Those are the long, crazy weeks."

"But you're enjoying it?" Randall seemed to love history and English, but something about the way he talked about them was slightly disconnected.

He shrugged and started playing with the menu half-heartedly. "It's not bad. And I like the subjects."

That wasn't much of an endorsement. "What do you plan on doing after you graduate?" Maybe if I understood his plans, the whole thing would make more sense.

"After my doctorate program?" He looked up and cocked his head. "Probably teach. That's what my parents think would be best."

It still seemed like an odd way to talk about his future. "What do you think? Does teaching sound fun?"

His brows came together, and his shoulders jerked in a half-shrug. "Maybe? I'm sure it won't be that bad."

I'd never met a teacher who went into it thinking it wouldn't be that bad. They were usually a passionate bunch. Several of the employees down at the warehouse had spouses who were teachers, and men or women, they were usually outspoken about their job. Love it or hate it, it was never that watered down.

"So it was your family's idea for you to teach?"

He nodded and started browsing through the burgers listed on the menu. "Business wasn't my thing, so they thought it would be a good idea."

They knew there weren't just two options, right?

Not wanting to step into a mess I didn't understand, I steered away from the discussion. "What looks good?"

"A burger."

Laughing, I nudged his foot with mine. "What kind looks good?"

He looked up and smiled. "They all do."

"Did you miss lunch too?"

His expression turned more thoughtful, and he looked like the conversation was finally starting to make sense. I would have loved to have heard what was going through his mind, but he wasn't ready to start sharing that with me. Not yet, anyway.

"Was work that crazy for you again today? Do you normally work this many hours?"

"No, I'm usually more of a nine-to-five paper pusher with the occasional work taken home. But we have a vacancy that seems to be impossible to get someone to fill, so I'm having to work two jobs. It's a small company, and there just aren't that many people who can do the job until someone else gets hired." As long as we could get someone in that position soon, I wouldn't go crazy. The long hours were starting to catch up with me, though.

"Isn't there someone you can ask to step in and help?" Randall set the menu down and started fiddling with his napkin. "Even on a temporary basis?"

"Not really. My dad ran things before I stepped in, and asking him for help seems wrong. He's retired and having a good time. I'm not going to ruin that. I don't think it's going to take much longer to get someone in there." I crossed my fingers and gave Randall a smile. "Then it will be back to regular hours."

Once I caught up. And got Wes a bonus. And did my duties at the party. Then everything could get back to normal.

He gave me a look like he didn't believe me, which smart of him, but dropped the subject. "I think the bacon one sounds good, what about you?"

I thought my arteries would shoot me, and my pants probably wouldn't fit tomorrow. The age difference wasn't going to drive me crazy, but there were some places where it would definitely show. "I think something a little less heartburn-inducing might be a good idea for me."

Randall grinned. "But it sounds so good."

The restaurant had an eclectic menu and most of it looked delicious, but I had enough going on that I wasn't going to keep myself up because of stupid decisions. "And I bet the seasoned fries and a milkshake do too?"

He nodded, and his smile made him look like a kid in a candy store. "That's even better. My mother likes to eat healthy, so we didn't have anything like this growing up. Most kids their freshman year were overwhelmed by the classes and studying, but I was in awe of the food."

I could just see a stunned young Randall wandering around the dining hall, trying to figure out what to eat first. He would have been adorable. "Ice cream three meals a day?"

"Who lets people do that?" Randall seemed like he still couldn't believe it. "They have a machine in the dining hall that serves it all the time."

He glanced away and got a shy look on his face. "It took me a while to talk myself into it."

It was easy to picture the conflicted boy walking by the ice cream, desperately wanting it, but not letting himself have it. I was betting that he was downplaying how hard it had been to get it the first time. "I'm glad you let yourself have it. Everyone needs to figure out for themselves what they like and what makes them happy."

Randall peeked up, and I could tell he knew I wasn't just talking about the food. Giving me a thoughtful look, he took a deep breath. "I'm starting to understand that."

So cute.

"It's not something you have to figure out on your own." We were definitely going too fast, but I just couldn't help it. And to be honest, I didn't see a reason to slow down. I alternated between wanting to wrap him up in my arms and bending him over my lap. Both would have been preferable.

He blushed faintly, and it was like the understanding confused him. He mumbled a low, "Thank you."

It was time for another topic. He looked like he needed some space to clear his head. "You mentioned your family, do you see them often?"

Maybe that wasn't as easy a topic as I thought, because his face got a pinched look, and he sighed. "They love me."

There was a big "but" coming after that statement. I hadn't meant for it to be a difficult subject.

"They just…always think they know best. And they're kind of overwhelming."

I wasn't sure if he meant the normal overbearing parent kind of behavior or something else. "Do they know you're gay?"

He nodded. "That wasn't a big surprise." Randall looked down at himself, then back up to me. "I look so manly and all."

"You look perfect." Had his parents given him some kind of complex?

Randall gave me a slightly sad smile and nodded. "My dad just pictured having a son to take over the family business. He was a football player in high school that went on to do big things and was…disappointed, I guess, that I was different than he expected."

Something about my expression must have gotten to Randall because he shook his head. "They're not mean, and they don't have an issue with me being gay. My mother even tried to fix me up with one of their friends' kids last year."

Was that how he got roped into a degree he didn't really want? Trying to please his parents?

"That's good. Mine were a little surprised when I came out in high school but didn't really care." They'd taken it in stride, and recently I'd started getting the "When are you going to bring home a nice man?" lectures. They didn't know about everything else. They were open and understanding, but there were some things you shouldn't share with family.

Spankings and BDSM were high on that list.

As we ordered and ate, the conversation bounced around to easier topics: movies he'd seen recently, plans for the winter holidays that would be coming up in a few months, he even talked about wanting to get an apartment, and shared that his mother was dead set against it. She seemed like a founding member of the helicopter parent brigade, that was never told she lost her rank when he went to college. I started to feel more grateful to my parents with every story he told.

By the time we finished dinner, we were both full, and he was relaxed and smiling. The tension and worry from earlier was gone, and I was starting to see the real Randall come through. The confident side of him that reminded me of the flirty twink I'd met at the bar, just without the sexy blushes and dirty old men egging him on.

"And then the professor came up behind him and slammed the book closed beside his head. The guy just about fell out of his chair. I know the ancient Asian history classes can be hard, but the professor does that to everyone who falls asleep in his class. We've all had at least three classes with the guy, so I just can't understand how people are still stupid enough to nod off in there." Randall's eyes were dancing with laughter. He was relaxed back in his seat and playing with the straw in his nearly empty milkshake.

"Maybe it was a late night at the strip club." I said it dryly, and Randall started to laugh.

"We're not really the party crowd. I'm not sure I can picture him with strippers."

"Who said he was watching? A lot of people strip through college to pay for tuition." I loved the way Randall's eyes would bug out of his head when I said something the least bit outrageous.

"He wouldn't..." He couldn't seem to move past the visual in his head. His gaze went foggy, and I could see the idea swirling around.

Was he thinking of the guy? Or picturing himself?

It could go either way, but my little exhibitionist was probably imagining himself up on that stage, pole in hand. "I could see you doing that."

His hand knocked his cup, almost sending the last dregs of his milkshake all over the table. "What?"

It came out loud enough and high-pitched enough that several people turned to make sure he was okay. His stunned expression clearly had them curious, but I thought his blush gave away the naughty thoughts running through his head.

"Don't tell me you've never imagined it. Up on the stage... everyone watching you...You'd look incredible." He couldn't seem to decide if I was teasing or not. But I was completely serious. It was so easy to picture him turning and writhing, that sexy ass framed by a jock that would barely cover his cock. His hard, aching cock.

"I...but...I..." One moment he was laughing and telling me stories about class, and the next, I'd fried his brain. He was so cute when he was turned on and startled.

It was so hard to remember I was supposed to be just getting to know him. Learning what turned him on was still knowledge. Yeah, I was gonna to go with that.

Randall shifted in his seat, probably trying to subtly adjust his growing erection, and seemed to be finally collecting his brain from where it had scattered all over the table. "But I couldn't...No...that would..."

Couldn't...not wouldn't. That was interesting.

"You don't have to if you don't find it interesting, but I think you would be incredible." He was clearly conflicted about the idea. His pupils were wide and his tongue kept flicking out to lick his lips, but it was impossible to miss the storm of emotion running through him. Doubt seemed to war with desire, and I was afraid the doubt would win.

"But wanting something like that...only people who...I just..." His thoughts came out rambling and broken, but it was easy to read between the lines.

I let my voice drop low, and I reached out to take his hand. It was shaky, and I could feel the tension in his body. "Wanting something like that isn't wrong and doesn't make you a bad person. You like to be watched. And the idea of having all those men leering at you and calling out dirty things makes you so hot you can't think. I find that incredibly erotic."

His brows came together, and his hand tightened in mine. "But wouldn't you...all those men..."

"Get jealous?" He nodded reluctantly, but I was glad he was able to ask me his questions. "No, because I would know you were coming home with me and that you were my boy. I'd tell you what you could do, and I'd pick out what you would wear...I'd make you practice just for me..."

Randall's eyes widened again, and his mouth dropped open, but he leaned toward me and I could tell how aroused he was getting, so I kept going. Bad Dom...Bad. "One night I'd spank you, make that fabulous ass nice and red, then send you up on stage. Everyone would know you'd been punished, but they would see how hard it made you, and would know you were my little slut."

For a moment, I thought I'd gone too far. He just sat there looking at me, shock and desire flashing through his eyes.

One word came out, breathy and filled with need. "Yes."

My dirty angel.

8

_____

RANDALL

I WASN'T sure how I'd gone from heaven to hell so quickly. Not that sitting in a public restaurant listening to Hudson's fabulously dirty imagination should probably be considered heaven, but it was to me. The insane things that had come out of his mouth had seemed so incredible...so possible. It was like he could see me up on that stage, and the idea didn't horrify him or send him running. He'd just found ways to make it even hotter.

How had he known?

I would never actually do something like that. My parents would've locked me up and then thrown away the key, but the fantasy was perfect and tempting. I wasn't an idiot. I knew real life wouldn't work the same way my fantasies did. But the fantasies were enough to make me wake up drenched in sweat and precum.

It was like he could see right inside me.

That should have scared the hell out of me, but for some reason, it just made me feel safe. If he could peek inside and wouldn't run, then it should be safe to actually share things with him...right?

"Rand? Are you paying attention?" The voice was too cultured to be shrill, but it came close.

"I'm sorry, Mother. My mind wandered." Too much sex on the brain. "You know how school is."

Hell should have been a burning inferno where the damned were punished. Not my mother's overly fussy dining room. The long, smooth table was stunning, but the layers of silverware and linens seemed to be designed to hide the simple beauty of the wood.

Nothing could be simple in her home.

"We do not require your presence very often. I'm sure you can drag yourself from your studies for a few minutes." My father looked up from the papers and files that crowded around his place setting. He always said *studies* like it was a disease. I still wasn't sure if he realized how he said it or not, but I'd long since given up caring.

Mostly.

"Becoming a doctor is hard work. It doesn't matter what kind." My mother had a different approach to my education. Any kind of a doctor would be good for the family tree, so she was going to embrace it and tell everyone how hard I worked, and what a good professor I would be.

I think she pictured me having tenure at Harvard, teaching something obscure, but I wasn't sure what I was going to do. Hudson's stripper idea was starting to sound more like a lucrative business plan every minute. "Thank you, Mother. I apologize for my mental wandering."

"That's alright, dear." Her pinched expression smoothed out to something more closely resembling maternal affection, but it was gone too soon. "I was just telling you about a lovely gentleman I met at the planning committee for the hospital charity ball."

Shit.

"How did the meeting go? Is it better run this time? I

remember last year you had problems with some of the newer members not stepping up to their responsibilities." I was hoping it would be enough to distract her. She'd had a fit last year when some of the younger wives with new money kept trying to change things.

No such luck.

"It's going fine." That lie rolled off her tongue, but the flash of frustration in her eyes gave her away. "But Dr. Richards is a pediatrician who works in the neonatal unit. He's very nice and was a wonderful conversationalist. He had some very good ideas for the party."

That probably translated to, "He let me talk about myself for hours and didn't argue with me about how I said things should be run."

Great.

"I'm glad you found new members who have the same vision you do for the foundation."

There was no dragging her away from the doctor. I could see the stubbornness setting in. "He's new to the area. He was working in California up until recently. He said he wanted to be closer to his family."

He was sounding less and less like a good catch—and that's where the conversation was heading.

We'd started going through this routine a little over a year ago. There seemed to have been some arbitrary deadline for picking out a partner that I'd missed, and she was making it her duty to find me someone. Preferably a man who was wealthy, boring, and in the same social circle she ran in.

Doctor and Doctor Whoever would be right up her alley.

Any man who worked with kids all day, got along with my mother, and wanted to live closer to *his* was probably a serial killer. They'd find my dead body buried in a shallow grave on the side of the interstate.

Someone kill me now.

"I'm sure his family appreciates it." Taking another bit of my too-tiny slice of quiche, I let my mind wander back to the cheeseburger from the night before. Bacon, and cheese, and fries, and words so hot they should have been in an X-rated movie.

That had been perfect.

A small piece of overcooked eggs and fruit that was almost too ripe wasn't anywhere close to perfect. My mother must have argued with the cook again. Mrs. Middleton was the only person in the world who wasn't intimated by my mother. She'd had enough offers to work for other families that unless my mother wanted to actually lose her, and my father would put his foot down there, she had to behave and stay out of the kitchen.

Given the sad state of the meal, they'd argued about Mother going on a diet again.

Mother was tiny and delicate-looking, and where I got my metabolism from, so she had to be constantly starving. But there was always something she was looking to change or some fad diet that looked interesting. It made Mrs. Middleton insane.

"He's going to be at the party next week, and I'll introduce you." She gave me a smile that looked surprisingly happy. "He seems very interested in meeting you. He said young men of good breeding are hard to find these days."

Fuck.

How old was the guy?

I was going to be sold off like a bride from one of those old stories, just so she could look better to her friends. Yes, her son was gay, but he was married to a doctor, so that made everything better. What the hell had she told him about me?

Good *breeding*?

What was I, a fucking horse?

Of course, none of that came out. I was a rebel in my head, though, so that had to count for something. "I'm sure there are lots of other men in the area for him to get to know. California may have had a bigger dating pool, but there are a variety of places he can meet people here."

Hopefully, someone who wasn't me.

I was kind of taken.

Probably taken.

That whole *you're mine* thing and actually taking me out in public on a real date seemed to point to me being taken. And then there was the domination part with me calling him Master…yup…probably taken. I just wasn't going to tell my mother that.

"I'm sure you'll find him enjoyable." She smiled over at my father, who wasn't listening. "I have good taste."

Fuck.

If he was anything like my dad, I was totally screwed. Stuffy, boring, convinced he was right, and so vanilla he'd probably never heard of anything remotely fun. Spankings? No. Letting me flirt and tease? Hell, no. I could picture my future now. Missionary sex once a week while I laid there and tried to be aroused just the right amount.

Too excited—I'm a slut. Too quiet—I'm a cold fish.

It would be art museums and Sunday brunches with the *right* kind of people forever.

Even in my head I sounded whiny. I just couldn't help it. There were a few people my parents knew that I actually enjoyed talking to and weren't painful to be around, but for the most part, I simply tolerated their acquaintances.

It'd been that way for years. For a long time, I'd been able to avoid it, but now that she thought I was finally an adult, or whatever was going through her head, she was starting to drag me to more of her events and get-togethers.

A few months ago, the last time I was cornered, I'd had to have dinner with some of their friends, and one of the daughters of a business associate of Dad's tried to keep flirting with me. She knew I was gay, but it was some kind of *let's see if we can make him straight* game or just her way of passing the time. Either way, I'd been miserable and there had been no way to escape.

This time would be even worse, I just knew it.

"I'm sure he'll have a wonderful time meeting more people. You know so many locals that he would probably enjoy being introduced to." She knew everyone who was anyone. It was tiresome.

I wasn't the only gay son mixed in with their friends. Maybe I could find someone else to get to know him. Someone who was actually boring, and not just really good at pretending to fit in.

She shook her head. "There is only one person I'm interested in introducing him to. He'll be snatched up before long if you drag your feet. When a man starts looking to get serious, it's obvious, and you have to catch his attention right then."

I was their sacrificial virgin daughter. Just one with a dick.

"I still have too much hard work to get serious now. My doctorate program is going to be very intense. I'm not sure it's fair to someone to get involved and then put them on the back burner." Like Dad had done to her for years.

I had to keep reminding myself that she seemed happy, and that it wasn't my marriage. Thank god.

"I'm sure he would understand. He had his own studies that took up an enormous amount of time. I'm sure he wouldn't begrudge yours." She was determined and knew she was right. It was too bad she was completely insane.

"I'll certainly be polite when you introduce us, but Mother, I'm not promising to date the man." It was as close as I was going to get to telling her no, and I could see the frustration starting to well up in her.

"We'll see. I'm sure he'll find you delightful," was all she said. Like that was the only thing that mattered.

My father chose that moment to chime in. Evidently, either his paperwork was done, or not as interesting as watching his son being sold off. "Men in his position have a difficult time finding a...partner who belongs in our social circles. He can't bring home some young punk he met at a club. Those...*people* are not the sort you marry."

And evidently, I was boring enough that I was the marrying type. Great.

HIDING IN MY DORM ROOM, WRAPPED IN MY COVERS WITH the TV on, I finally felt like I could relax. They didn't make me go home often, thank god, but when they did, it seemed to take everything out of me. On those days, studying didn't get done, and I avoided the real world as much as possible for the rest of the day.

My recuperative obsession of choice for that terrible day was bad fast food that was rapidly getting colder and a marathon on the History Channel about the worst serial killers in history. Not the healthiest combination, but it was perfect for distracting my brain from everything else that was bubbling inside. Besides, there weren't any Law and Order marathons on.

When my phone buzzed halfway through the show, I frowned and silently cursed the fact that it was on my dresser. It seemed very far away. If it was someone from school or my family, I wasn't going to even think about answering the phone, but the idea that it might be Hudson was too tempting.

Pushing away the half-eaten burger, I crawled out of my covers and went over to see who was calling. *Hudson*. The sigh of relief that escaped me was probably ridiculous, but he was the only person I wanted to talk to, and just seeing his name on my phone made me feel better.

I was totally insane and rapidly going head over heels for him, but I couldn't help it.

"Hello?" I may have sounded a little bit desperate.

"Lunch didn't go well?" His voice was soothing and warm. There wasn't the usual trace of naughty teasing that made me squirm, but the concern and tenderness made me feel special.

I sighed and walked back over to the bed, pushing away the wrappers so I could curl up again. "No."

"Do you want to talk about it?" It honestly felt like he would actually listen.

"Not really. You talk to me." The offer was sweet, but describing my family would sound like the poor little rich kid whining. The few times I'd tried to vent to people, it hadn't gone well. Money meant happiness, and when you had money you were supposed to ignore the crazy.

Money didn't fix everything and didn't make your parents understand you.

"Well, I'm on my way over to my parents' house. I missed dinner last week, and if I miss it again, they're going to chase me down and see what the problem is." He laughed, but I could hear the concern in his voice.

"You should just talk to them. Your dad might have a good idea about hiring someone." Hudson's parents seemed functional. Real people, who didn't care who their son slept with and were proud of him.

Hudson sighed, and I had to bite back a giggle. "You can't be logical too."

"I'm assuming Wes gave you that speech as well?" There was no hiding the laughter in my voice that time.

"Yes, several times this week." Hudson was quiet for a moment, and I could picture him, fingers tapping on the wheel while he thought. He was a fidgeter when he drove, and it was cute. "I'll think about it. But only if we haven't found any good candidates to interview by the end of the week. I'm not just being stubborn."

He was reading my mind again.

"If it was something important, then I would call him. This is just extra hours and some inconvenience. It's not a make-or-break problem for the company. It's one position. It shouldn't be this hard to fill." He was starting to get frustrated, and I didn't want him to be upset. I liked that he could talk to me about it.

"Did I tell you about the other applicants we initially had for the job? One ended up in jail. He was stealing from his old company, and he's accused of a physical assault on another employee as well. I know there are better people in the neighborhood, but I'm just not finding them." His frustration was mounting, and I just wanted to find something that would help.

"Maybe they just don't think they're qualified or good enough. People won't try for something that looks too good to be true." It was too hard when they were repeatedly shot down and felt stupid.

Hudson's voice was soft, and there was something in it I couldn't describe. "Not unless they are very brave. But you're right; maybe it looks harder than it really is. I'll talk to Wes about the job description."

"I knew a finance major last year who was looking around at jobs and found one that seemed perfect, but the qualifications were weird and the description was confusing. It talked about geometry and all kinds of math no one had used since high school, nothing that seemed to have anything to do with the job. She took a chance and applied. It turned out, the HR department had just copied and pasted the description from something they'd found online. They didn't even realize the math stuff was listed. It scared off so many people that there were only a handful of applicants."

"Did she get the job?" I could hear the smile in Hudson's

voice. The story wasn't that funny, but none of us had been able to figure out why the job needed to know the area of a circle.

"Yup. She's living in Texas or someplace down there."

Hudson laughed. "I'll make sure there isn't any weird math listed."

"You never know. Maybe you have some kind of typo that says they have to be able to stand on their head and say the alphabet backward." It was the hardest thing that came to mind right away.

His chuckle sent shivers down my spine. "I'm not sure anyone can do that."

"I knew a guy my freshman year who could do that. But only when he was drunk. Not sober." I'd met interesting people at school. Far more interesting than I'd led my parents to believe. It was too bad they couldn't relate to me. Different only seemed good when it involved drinking or weird skills like being able to wiggle their nose like that old TV witch.

"I'll take your word on that." The stress was gone from his voice, and he seemed lighter than when he'd first called. "I'm almost at the house, but I just wanted to know if you wanted to come by my house later. Dessert and a movie?"

"What kind of dessert?" Real dessert or the naughty kind?

"That's a surprise. But I'll let you pick out the movie."

"Deal." I was up for *whatever* he was planning. He might constantly surprise me, but I had a feeling that nothing I did would surprise him.

9

―――――

HUDSON

"YOU'VE BEEN WORKING TOO HARD. You're tired." My
mother's hovering was at Olympic level before I'd even walked
in the door. I knew I looked rough, but it wasn't nearly as bad
as she was making it out to be.

It was *not* dreams of work that kept me up last night.

"I'm fine. You just worry." Giving her a kiss, I looked
toward the door. "Do I get to come in and eat?"

She gave a sniff and frowned at me. "I don't see you for two
weeks, and now all you want is food." Leaning close, she looked
suspicious. "Who is he? Not enough sleep...not enough food...
you've met someone."

Crazy woman with ESP.

Lying was bad. She'd spot it a mile away. "You'd prefer to
interrogate your only son instead of feeding him? Where's Dad?
He wouldn't grill me. Where's Mama Sylvia? She loves me."

That distracted her, but not in the way I'd hoped; one
eyebrow went up and her lips pinched together. "Sylvia has the
week off. If you'd been here last time when you were supposed
to be, you would know that. Her sister fell, and she went home
to see how she's doing."

And I was going to get a guilt trip for months over this.

Oh well, that was better than being quizzed about my sex life. I wasn't hiding Randall. I just wasn't ready to share him yet, and I wasn't sure where he thought we were going. It constantly seemed to surprise him that I wasn't trying to shove him in a closet like my dirty secret. Until I really got through to him and made sure we were both on the same page, I couldn't bring him home.

And telling my mother vague details about a guy I might be serious about was dangerous. She was part bloodhound. "Is Aunt Trina okay?"

Sylvia had been working for our family since I was born. I didn't remember a time when she wasn't around. My mother liked to tease that Sylvia was my first word. She was more family than anything else and had been Mama Sylvia forever.

"She'll be fine. Just overdoing it for a woman her age." Mama started heading into the house, shaking her head like she just couldn't believe the outrageous behavior Aunt Trina had been up to. "And it's giving Sylvia a vacation. She thinks with your father here all the time, we need more supervision."

I completely agreed with Sylvia, but I was smart enough not to say it.

"We're staying busy." As I shut the front door, Mama led me in through the house toward the kitchen. "Your father is finishing up something on TV. A golf match, I think. I'm not sure."

She glanced back toward his study. "If I go in and actually see what he's doing, he'll make me stay and watch. I had to sit through an entire game…match…whatever it's called last week. You can go see what he's up to, if you're interested."

Um, no thanks. "I'll see what you've got going in the kitchen."

She laughed and gave me a knowing look. Neither of us got Dad's infatuation with golf or really sports in general. I had fun playing sports in high school and college, but sitting on the couch for a couple of hours watching other people play wasn't my thing. Much to Dad's utter disappointment.

"Good idea." She continued on through the living room and into the kitchen. The place was too big for just them, but it had been their home for most of their marriage, so I knew they'd never move out. With their suite of rooms at one end of the massive structure, and Sylvia's at the other, the house could have boarded a small army. It was home, though.

I'd grown up sliding down the massive wood staircase on couch cushions and playing the best games of hide-and-seek with my friends. It could have felt cold and sterile, but it was filled with memories and love.

"You finish the salad for me. I'm going to check on dinner." She pointed to the half-finished salad on the table and went over to the stove. Watching her stirring things and moving pots around, I wasn't sure what she'd made, but it smelled like curry.

When Sylvia was home, the kitchen was her domain, but when she was out of town, Mom loved to try out new recipes. When Sylvia had gone on a cruise with her family when I was in high school, we'd had a different soup every night for the two weeks she had been gone. Dad and I had been desperate for Sylvia to come back.

"The kitchen looks good." As I started cutting up vegetables, I looked around the room. They'd recently had it renovated. It'd turned out great, a more updated version of the room I'd grown up with. They'd kept the same layout, so there was still room for the large island as well as the long table, but the new cabinets and tilework brought it all together.

"I think so too." She smiled, satisfied and pleased. "When he said he was ready to tackle the renovation, I thought he was crazy, and I'd end up with a partially done mess, but it turned out wonderfully."

"What's he thinking of doing next?" I thought the house

looked fine, but Dad thought that it was showing its age and had a list of things that had to be done. He kept talking about leaving a legacy for my future children and giving me pointed looks. He was as bad as she was.

"The downstairs bathrooms." She started shaking her head. "I told him it was going to have to wait until after the party. I'm not living in a mess and trying to finalize all those details too."

"So what's he going to do instead?" I knew them both well enough to be able to read between the lines.

"Our bathroom." She sighed and kept tinkering with the pots on the stove. "I got what I wanted, but I think I lost that battle."

"Oh, yeah." Yup, I'd have let him mess with the guest bathrooms. But she was right; he wouldn't be able to get everything done before the party. No matter how good the contractors were. "I thought you guys were going to head down to the beach early this year? With all these projects, are you still planning on it?"

"I'm not sure yet." Worry passed over her face. "I think it's going to be a while before he's ready."

"Everything okay?"

"Yes. He's just restless, I think." She put down the spoon she'd been using and went over to the cabinets. Getting out plates and cups, she started setting the table. "I knew it was going to be a bit of a transition for him. He's worked full-time since he was a young man."

"You guys talked about traveling." They'd had a list of things that they'd wanted to do, but so far, they hadn't done much. Just golf and renovations.

"That's partly my fault. I thought I'd be ready to step down from my committees, but there are a few big projects that I'm working on, and I'm not willing to turn them over to someone else yet. Maybe once we have everything finalized for the new children's wing at the hospital, and the new library built."

People might scoff at the image of the rich wife who played with charities, but my mother put the *work* in charity work. She might never have taken a salary for what she'd done, but there was plenty of time growing up where she'd been just as busy as my father. She took her positions very seriously.

"I can understand that." Dad had wanted to pull back on the number of hours he'd been working, and giving me the space to take over was at the forefront of his mind. But he was too active to sit around doing nothing. "Has he thought about volunteering or joining you with some of your charities?"

She looked over at the door to the kitchen and frowned. "Bite your tongue. I love your father dearly, but being retired does not mean he has to live in my back pocket. It's like having a teenager home for the summer already. I'm not taking him to work."

Laughing probably wasn't the right response, but it was too perfect. "I'm sorry. I won't mention it again."

She waved a finger at me, still keeping one eye on the door. "If you do, I'm telling him you're overstressed and need his help at work. I'm not above fighting dirty."

I knew she was teasing, but she hit a little too close to home. I tried to play it off. "That's just mean."

I got a sassy grin from her. "Where do you think you learned it from?"

"Whatever it is, I'm sure you're guilty, my dear." I was saved as Dad came in the room, his deep voice booming. "You are a bad influence."

She gave him an innocent smile and shook her head. "I have no idea what you're talking about."

"Of course you don't." He gave her an indulgent smile.

They'd been married for more than forty years, but he still looked at her like they were newlyweds. She was tall for a woman, but as he came up and wrapped his arms around her, trapping her against the counter, he towered over her.

She always said his good looks gave him a leg up in the boardroom. He just brushed it off and said it was merely his charm and good *luck* that had the business going so well. Since I looked like a younger version of him, I was hoping they were both right. Looks, charm, and good luck would be a wonderful combination to keep the company going in the right direction.

———

"ANGEL, YOU'RE FINALLY HERE." THROWING THE DOOR OPEN, I reached out and pulled Randall into my arms. I wasn't going for subtle or playing it cool. I needed to show him he was wanted.

He grinned and looked slightly bashful, like he wasn't sure what to do with my enthusiasm. "You saw me last night."

"And it was a very long night without you." Tugging him close, I didn't hide my excitement. I wasn't going to make him guess how he affected me. He wasn't some overconfident twink who wanted to play games. He needed more than that. "You kept me up all night."

He blinked up at me, shy and a little confused. "I did?"

"I had wicked dreams about my dirty angel." I whispered the words and watched as he blushed, and a shiver ran through him. "Very wicked dreams."

"*Oh.*" The word was soft and filled with desire.

"I'm going to have to punish you for keeping me up like that." His eyes got wide, and he rocked his body against mine. The hard cock that pressed against my body let me know the direction his thoughts were going. "But not tonight."

"Oh?" Now he sounded distinctly disappointed, a little frown starting to form.

Unable to resist, I leaned down and gave him a quick, tender kiss. "I promised you dessert and a movie tonight."

His tongue came out to lick his lips, and he looked up at me hungrily. "Yes, dessert."

Keeping my hands to myself was going to be impossible. He was too tempting and too needy. As much as I'd tormented both of us last night, he hadn't asked to come. And as honest as his submission was, I knew he would do his best to follow my instructions. Knowing how hard he was, and how long it had been since he'd come, pushed my arousal even higher.

Giving him one last chaste kiss, I stepped back and took one of his hands. "Treat. Then we'll pick out the movie."

Randall looked like his brain was having a hard time keeping up. "Um, what kind?"

Thinking that he was referring to the food, because that was where my mind was going, I answered him. "I picked up a couple of kinds of ice cream."

It was simple, as far as desserts went. However, it was my favorite.

"More than one?" That seemed to shock him just as much as my going after him in the bar the first night. He stopped in his tracks before we made it through the living room and just looked at me.

"Of course." Stopping at one seemed incredibly wrong. How were you supposed to narrow down how you'd feel two or three nights later when you were standing in the frozen food section?

"Sometimes it's a rocky road kind of night, and sometimes you just want plain chocolate. And every once in a while vanilla calls, so you have to have that too." I was being fairly serious, but he looked at me like I was insane.

Had I picked the wrong dessert?

"Are you allergic? I have some brownie mix in the cabinet. We can make that instead." Those were good too, and as long as he didn't mind, I could have that with ice cream. Hmm, not a bad idea.

"Allergic? No." Still the same cute, confused expression.

"Do you like ice cream? You won't hurt my feelings. I might question your sanity, but I can learn to live with it. Even my angel can't be completely perfect." He finally cracked a smile, but he still seemed shocked.

"I like ice cream." Well, we were finally getting somewhere.

"See, you are perfect." Figuring I'd eventually understand what was going on with the dessert crisis in his head, I gave him another peck on the lips and started pulling him toward the kitchen.

He was like a car that needed a push to get going. Once I had him moving, his brain started kicking in. "I like your house."

"Thank you." I'd found the small one-bedroom condo in a great part of town a few years ago and had snatched it up right away. It didn't have a lot of extra space, and sometimes the layout was funny, but it was beautiful.

The area was mostly filled with brownstone-style buildings like you would see up north, but a handful of them had been converted into condos and apartments. The prices were still crazy when you compared it to apartments in other parts of the city, but I loved it.

"It's a little small, but it works for me." I smiled as I dragged him into the kitchen. "My mother thinks I live in a closet. It makes her crazy."

"For some reason, I think that's part of the appeal for you." He grinned and started looking around the room.

"You're right. That's what sons are for."

His smile dimmed. "Not in my family."

"That's not as much fun, then." Looking around, I wasn't sure where he should stand. It was a tiny kitchen. The area had originally been a large closet or part of a hallway, it was hard to tell. The previous owners had renovated it with nice cabinets and granite countertops, but there wasn't much they could do about the layout or the space.

On two walls, there was an L-shaped area with the stove on one end and the fridge on the other. It wasn't bad, and I actually had a window that looked out over the shared back garden. I would have probably put a table on the other wall, but the previous owners thought storage was more important than an eat-in kitchen, so they'd put another wall of lower cabinets with shelves going up the wall.

I thought it just made the room feel more cluttered, but my mother thought it was designed beautifully. And I had to admit the extra storage was great. The tight floor plan and limited space were not wonderful, however.

"Come here, Angel. Hop up."

"Wha—" He gave a high-pitched squeak as I picked him up and plopped him down on the counter.

"There we go." His eyes were still wide, and he was a little breathless. He looked like we'd been making love. I was *never* going to manage to behave. He was too tempting.

Giving him another kiss, I let my hands rest on his thighs, just high enough to tease at the head of his dick, which was now outlined against the stiff fabric of the jeans. He wasn't wearing the tight, sexy ones, but sitting down, even the loose pants couldn't hide his arousal.

Randall moaned and leaned into me, and his hands started tracing up my arms. Knowing we would get too easily distracted if we kept it up, I ran my thumb over the tip of his dick and stepped back. His body shook, and his eyes went all confused and foggy again. He was so sensitive and so open with his need, it felt wrong to pull away.

But I had to at least try to stick to the plan. If I didn't, he'd end up naked and orgasming. And I wanted him needy and completely on edge by the time he went back to work. His punishment had to be something he would remember forever.

"What kind of ice cream, Angel?" He just blinked at me. Nothing. "Angel? I need my sexy boy to tell me what he wants to eat."

"You."

Fuck. It was going to be a long night.

10

RANDALL

I HADN'T MEANT to say that. Chocolate. That was what I'd tried to say. It just hadn't come out that way. I would have felt stupid, but the look on Hudson's face just made me even more turned on. He liked the idea.

He took one step closer and moved his hands back to grip my thighs. But when he shook his head, I couldn't help but feel like I'd said something wrong. "Did I…"

"Oh, Angel, you say the—" Hudson's mouth took mine in an aggressive kiss that felt more like a claim than the sweeter pecks he'd given me earlier. I just sank into him and opened, letting him have whatever he wanted. His tongue slid against mine, and all I could picture was how it would feel to have that wet heat wrapped around lower things.

By the time he pulled away, I was dizzy, and my cock was so hard it ached. Hudson moved one hand to cup my face, his expression still making it clear how turned on he was, but there was also something tender I couldn't define. "I am going to have an evening in with my boy. We're going to watch TV and have ice cream. I'm going to kiss you and touch you…" The hand on my leg moved so he could tease the tip of my cock again. "But you're not going to get to come."

What?

His smiled turned wicked. "I want to get to know you more. *With our clothes on*. If you're good, though, I might give you some hints about your punishment later this week. I don't feel bad admitting how much I'm looking forward to it."

The slow caress of his fingers and the dirty words coming out of his mouth made it hard to think. "Punish?"

I wasn't sure that's what I'd meant to say, but that was what came out. Hudson leaned in and flicked his tongue over my lips, more like he tasted me than actually kissed me, but it was even hotter somehow. "Yes, Angel. I want you to be nice and ready for my punishment. So no coming this week. Do you understand?"

Fuck.

"I…I…" There were just no words.

His face lit up with a dark desire, and I knew how much he loved my reaction. Blowing my mind seemed to be something he *thoroughly* enjoyed. "But no…"

That hadn't been an actual question, but we both knew what I was trying to say. It'd felt like I was a walking hard-on most days, and the idea of not being able to orgasm until…until he punished me was insane. I just couldn't figure out if it was the bad kind of crazy or the good kind.

"No playing with that sexy cock. No humping the bed, pretending that I'm taking that sexy ass. No teasing that little hole until you come." His hand started sliding up and down my dick as he talked, and I couldn't hold back the moan that tore through me. "Nothing at all. Do you understand, Angel?"

"No…" I knew he'd asked a question, but all I could focus on was the wicked pictures he'd put in my head. "I can't…"

I realized that I'd agreed to him having control of my orgasms, but I'd just never imagined how hot it would be when he said no. I hadn't actually figured out how to ask him yet, so I was already on edge, but knowing he was asserting that control had my cock jerking and precum leaking out. Wet jeans were going to be the least of my problems, though.

"Master?"

"Yes, Boy." That tender look was back, but it was still wrapped in the same desire that radiated from him. "You're going to stay nice and hard for me, aren't you?"

I nodded, words still beyond me.

"If you're good tonight, and then take your punishment well, I'll give you a reward." The way he said it had flames of desire flashing through me.

Reward meant orgasm, right?

An orgasm without me having to ask might be worth the wait. I'd tried to text him several times, but I hadn't been able to hit the button to send the message. It'd seemed...dirty...not wrong, exactly, because nothing he did felt bad, but just...too hard.

"I'll be good." The words came out low and almost husky. Hudson leaned in and gave me a gentle kiss, but didn't release my dick, so the combination made my head spin.

"I know you will." As he pulled away, he moved his hand back down my leg. I missed his touch, but it made it easier to think.

That wasn't really a good thing, because all I could focus on was that it was going to be days before I got to come again. Shit.

"Now, you were going to tell me what kind of ice cream you wanted."

I was?

"Um..." What were the choices again? "Can I have chocolate *and* vanilla?"

It felt greedy to ask for both, but it was what I wanted.

"Of course." He smiled like it was nothing to ask for both.

As he walked away, I immediately missed his touch, but my perch on the counter gave me an incredible view of his kitchen and his body.

Pulling my gaze away from his tempting strength, I tried to focus on something less likely to make me come in my pants. His kitchen was tiny, but every inch of space was being used, and I liked it. It was nothing like what I was used to, no flashy decorations or random pots just for show, but it felt warm and homey.

The rest of the house felt the same way. Well, the parts that I'd seen. The living room was filled with a big couch along one wall, and a TV on the opposite wall. The far side of the room had built-in shelves that had books and pictures on them. It was nothing like my dorm room or my parents' house, and that made it even better. I just wished it had been light enough when I'd gotten out of the cab to see the outside of the building.

Hudson had offered to come by and pick me up, but I'd had a few assignments that needed to be done, and I hadn't been sure how long they would take. Having a car would have made it easier, but that was another discussion I'd lost with Mother.

He chattered about his dinner with his parents and the errands he'd run that day while he scooped the ice cream out. Watching him pile it into the bowls shocked me. They were nothing like the dessert cups my mother used.

After he put everything away, he brought the bowls over and set them beside me on the counter. I got another kiss. They were addicting. "Do you know what movie you want to see?"

There were a few history documentaries out that I wanted to watch, but I figured there was at least a fifty-fifty shot that they would bore him to tears, so I tried to think of something else. "Do you have cable?"

Living in the dorms, I knew that was a crapshoot. Some people were on such a strict budget that they didn't have anything, even a TV. I wasn't sure what Hudson would have, although the house seemed nice, and the way he talked about the business made me think it was doing well.

He nodded. "A thousand channels of nothing, plus on-demand movie channels and several subscription sites."

That made it even harder to think of something. I shrugged. "Let's flick through some of the channels and see what's on."

I wasn't really there for the TV, anyway.

"Sounds like a plan." He reached out and helped me off the counter, letting his hands trail up my sides. He was so close, I slid down the front of his body and our cocks rubbed together. He might not let me come, but he was going to have fun torturing me.

I loved it.

Curled up on the wide, deep couch, we browsed through until we found an action movie that neither of us had seen. It was alright, but the best part was curling up next to Hudson and snuggling while we ate. When we were both done, he set the bowls on the coffee table and pulled me onto his lap.

I couldn't figure out how I was supposed to watch the movie with his cock pressing against my ass. Images of him bending me over the couch and fucking me flashed through my mind, only to be replaced with sexy images of him making love to me as his hands started slowly caressing me.

When his free hand started trailing up and down my legs, I thought it was just an unconscious habit. When his other hand began caressing up and down my side slowly, I thought he didn't understand how insane he was making me. When the hand on my leg started tracing circles around the head of my cock, I knew he understood *exactly* what he was doing.

I didn't want him to stop, but I didn't want to disobey him by coming, so I wasn't sure what to do. His touch always changed up the pleasure before it got to be too much, but I was leaking precum so badly there was a wet spot on my jeans, and there was a huge chunk of the movie that didn't make sense.

Not enough blood in my brain to follow the action.

When I finally broke, a whimper escaping as I started to shake, he gave a low, wicked laugh. "No coming, Boy."

It was that rough voice that I was starting to associate with him being Master, not just my…boyfriend…whatever we were. One moment he would be teasing and talking, then something would change and he'd suddenly be in charge and making me whine with need.

It was so crazy hot.

When he finally pulled his hand away from my cock, I let out a desperate sound, but he just chuckled and slid his hand up under my shirt. "Watch the movie, Angel."

It was the same voice he'd used to call me his dirty angel, and it sent a flood of emotion through me. Words like that shouldn't make me feel romantic and special, but somehow they did. His hot hand on my chest chased away everything but the need.

As he started circling my nipples with his fingers, I gave up pretending to watch the movie. I just closed my eyes and soaked up the pleasure of his touch. He would get closer, and then move farther away. It was maddening.

By the time he actually ran his thumb over my nipple, I was desperate, and there was no way to hide the mess I'd made of my jeans. It was embarrassingly erotic and just made it harder to get my body under control. Every time I thought about the evidence of my arousal, I got even more turned on, which made the problem worse.

"My dirty angel made a mess of his pants." He pinched my now overly sensitive tip and growled the words out. I knew my face was so red it was probably purple, but I didn't want to cover it up. It was wicked and naughty, but I was his dirty angel…he didn't want me to hide anything from him.

"I…it's just…I…" He moved his hand and pinched the other bud.

"Beautiful." His mouth took mine in a long kiss. His tongue dueled mine, and it was like he was fucking my mouth. "I'm not sure I can let you go home like this, though. Everyone would know what you were doing tonight."

Horror and arousal flashed through me.

The idea was…shocking, but there was no way I could go through the doors like that. No matter how erotic the fantasy was. "I guess you're just going to have to stay the night so I can wash those wet pants. I bet your briefs are just as wet, aren't they?"

I nodded and shook as he flicked my nipples with his finger, going back and forth, keeping my entire body humming with need. "Let's get you cleaned up."

Huh?

His hands moved out from under my shirt and I missed his touch immediately. "I don't…" I forced my eyes open and looked around, confused. The credits were rolling, and Hudson was watching me, his eyes dark with desire.

When had the movie finished?

He started to help me stand, but my legs didn't really work, so he wrapped his arms around me while I found my balance. Once I was steady, he moved one hand down to cup the wet front of my pants. It usually didn't get that bad. The precum only started to drip out when I was just about ready to come. But he'd had me needy and aching for so long, I hadn't been able to help it.

"I have some pants you can sleep in, and I'll wash your clothes, dirty boy." Desire filled his voice, and he didn't try to hide how much he loved my reactions to his touch. "Do you want to clean up by yourself, or do you want your master to wash your sticky, wet cock?"

Fuck.

I knew there was a question somewhere in his words, but it was lost in the images that were flashing through my head.

"Angel, do you want me to strip you down and clean you?"

"Yes." The word sounded husky and desperate, not like me at all.

"Good boy." Pleasure lit up his face, and it wasn't just about the desire.

He kept a tight grip on me as we walked down a small hallway toward what had to be his bedroom. My brain was short-circuiting, but I thought I saw a small half-bath to one side of the hall before he ushered me into his room. Hudson didn't seem to trust my legs, because he kept a tight hold on me and led me right to the bathroom.

The lights were bright after the darkness of his bedroom, which only had light coming from the street lamps outside the windows. His bathroom was entirely white, and what drew my attention was a large mirror over the sink.

My eyes were wide, and I looked…out of it…not quite drunk but clearly wrecked. Hudson stayed close as he watched me in the mirror, his hands moving to start taking off my clothes. As he stripped me down, gently and slowly, I thought it would be erotic, and it was…but there was a tenderness I hadn't expected. It made me feel almost vulnerable.

I would have thought that nothing would have been more intimate than his watching me orgasm, but as he bared my body in the mirror, I knew I was wrong. It was…incredible. I didn't know how to explain it. The need and desire were still there. I was hard and aching, but there were layers of other emotions I didn't understand.

When I was naked and wrapped in his arms, he reached out and grabbed a washcloth from the counter. I watched his hand move to turn the water on, and it was like I was watching it happen to someone else. As he brought the warm, wet cloth up to my chest, everything was hitting me in flashes. The soft feel of the fabric as it dragged over my skin. The touch of his clothed body as it pressed against my naked one. The sight of us in the mirror. It was completely overwhelming.

Intimate.

Special.

More than I'd ever dreamed of having with anyone.

As the washcloth went over my still-hard cock, carefully cleaning the precum that had soaked through my clothes, it only made everything harder to process. Hudson's face was so intent, and his touch so sure and gentle, I felt like something precious. Like one of the expensive figurines that required the most delicate touch.

He started whispering low words about how beautiful I was, and how much he loved to hold me. How he wanted to know everything about me. Eventually, he led me out of the bathroom, and I lost track of the words and just soaked up the sound of his voice as I forced my legs to work.

Dressing me in pants that were too big, I watched, still detached, as he tightened the string on the thin silky pants and tucked me into his bed. I still felt disjointed and only half real, but when he stripped down to his boxers, giving me the first hint of the hard cock I'd only felt through his clothes, my hands itched to touch him…to hold him.

Hudson slid under the covers and wrapped me in his arms, turning us so my head rested on his chest. I felt his naked skin for the first time. Letting my fingers trail over his chest as he held me tight, I closed my eyes and just let his heat sink into me.

"That's better. Sweet boy." His words were warm and loving. I hated to use the word…it felt too soon…but there was no other way to describe it. "My sweet boy."

My lids were heavy, so I let my fingers see as I traced his pecs and down to his hard abs. He was broad and wide, and his skin seemed to go on forever. His words got softer as he spoke, telling me how he liked holding me and feeling my touch.

"You're all mine, Angel." I wasn't sure if the reminder was for me or for him, but the words wrapped me in warmth.

"Yes, Master. I'm yours, Hudson." A yawn cracked my jaw, and my hand started to slow its exploration, but I wasn't ready to stop. My brain seemed to have other plans, though, because it got harder and harder to think.

"If I'm yours...that makes you mine...right?"

His low words wound their way through the fog in my head, fighting against the darkness that was pulling at me. The last thing I heard before I lost the battle was his deep voice, thick with what I wanted to call love. "Yes, Angel. I'm yours."

11

HUDSON

"YOU'VE MADE everyone in this whole damned place crazy," Jake grumbled as he wiped down the bar. "They're barely drinking."

"Not my fault."

"Bullshit. It's your boy they're waiting on. Normally, they'd be on their second rounds by now. But you've got them so worked up and excited, they don't even want a drink." Jake gave me a long stare that I tried to ignore. "I've been asked a dozen times already if I know what's going on with you two."

"Do you really want to know?" I wasn't going to hide it. Everyone would know in just a few minutes.

I'd taken off work early to be at the bar before Randall's shift started. It had been completely worth the crazy hours I'd worked the last two days to make sure I could be there before he walked in. Somehow, the men must have known it was a night he would be there, because the place was packed, and I knew some of the men weren't even supposed to be off work yet.

Everyone held their breath waiting for Randall, giving me

curious glances as I sat at the bar playing with a Coke. I'd switch to something else as the night wore on, but I wanted everything sharp when Randall walked in.

It was time for my boy's punishment.

We'd had a good time Sunday. I'd made him breakfast, and we'd just hung out until it was time for him to go back to the dorms. I hadn't pushed things too far, and we'd had a nice morning together. The rest of the week, I hadn't been so good.

I might have driven him a little bit crazy.

When he'd hinted that he was curious about his punishment, I'd told him all the ways I might do it. When he'd asked me how my day went, I'd told him all about how I'd fantasized about him that morning. It was more information that he'd been asking for, but he hadn't told me to stop. I'd just listened to his heavy breathing and the low whimpers that had escaped as he'd gotten more and more turned on.

My boy was ready to explode.

Luckily for him, it was finally time.

"I want to know." Andrew sighed dramatically and propped his head up on his hands, giving me a beseeching look. He was as curious as a cat, and had no patience when it came to watching Randall. Being able to drive Jake crazy might have had something to do with that, though.

"Are you sure?" I glanced over to see how far Jake was from us. Perfect. There was no way he would miss what I would say. "I know how you like my boy's ass. Do you really want to know what I'm going to do to it?"

Andrew practically purred. "Oh, yes, fuck, you have to—" The words stopped, and a low moan escaped as Jake did something behind his back. I heard a smack, but it had to have been good, because it nearly took Andrew's breath away.

Jake leaned in and whispered something quietly in his ear, and Andrew nearly melted into the bar. "Yes…please…"

They were giving everyone a show, but it was exactly what Andrew wanted because his eyes had lit up, and he was arching back, trying to get more of whatever Jake was doing. I wasn't sure if Jake knew his boy was getting him all wound up on purpose or not, but Andrew loved it. He was going to love it even more when Randall finally arrived.

Jake was going to have his hands full later.

The low buzz of the men in the bar dropped down to a whisper, and I knew it had to be Randall. Glancing across the room, I saw him standing in the doorway. As he walked in, I could feel him practically vibrating with excitement and energy. He was dressed in the baggy jeans I'd gotten used to seeing and plain black T-shirt that made him look even smaller. And younger.

The men ate it up, but I could tell what they really wanted was him in his uniform. I had to agree with them. I was ready to see those tight pants, too. He looked around, searching the room, and I could see it on his face went he finally found me.

With wide eyes dripping with desire, and a cock that was hidden, but I knew would be hard as a rock, he walked over, nervous and slightly unsure. I leaned back against the wall where I'd been waiting and gave him a devilish grin and crooked my finger.

When he was standing between my legs, holding on to his backpack straps with a white-knuckled grip, I reached out and trailed one finger from his neck to his belt. Every man in the room was silent, and I knew they were desperately trying to hear what would happen.

"It's been a long week, hasn't it, Angel?" I started caressing the edge of his pants, and I knew it was making him crazy.

He nodded, and it took a moment before he could get the words out. "Yes, Master."

The room was filled with excitement and curiosity. There

was a hum of voices as the men who'd heard Randall's words whispered to those who hadn't. Nosy old men.

"You've been very good this week. But I still have to punish you because you were naughty, weren't you?"

A needy whimper escaped as he nodded, but he couldn't seem to make his brain work because no words came out.

"Are you ready for your punishment, Angel?" Another jerky nod had me cupping his face and pulling him close. "I'm going to enjoy teaching you a lesson, Boy. Does that excite you, knowing you're going to turn me on?"

The most perfect little needy sounds escaped, but he nodded again. So turned on but so worried everything would come crashing down around him. "Does it excite you that they're all going to see? They're going to know you were naughty."

Another breathy moan escaped, but it was a good few seconds before he slowly nodded. So fuckin' sweet. "Good boy. Now, because you were honest with me, and because you were so good this week, I'm going to give you a reward later."

I'd let him stew over the reward for a while, but it was time to start his punishment. I pointed to his backpack. "Does that have your uniform in it?"

"Yes." It came out husky and shy, but it felt like he was starting to get his confidence back.

"Good. Then let's go in back and you can change. I have something you need for your punishment, Angel." A shiver raced through him, but he nodded and took a step away from me.

Standing, I grabbed the small bag I'd set on the counter and reached out to wrap my arm around him, guiding him toward the changing room. I let my hand rest possessively on his ass, kneading one cheek as we walked through the bar. Normally, the bar would have been too loud to hear the low gasp that caught in his chest, but we had every eye on us, and it was so quiet I could have heard a pin drop.

By the time we reached the employee bathroom, Randall's breathing was heavy, and I could feel the tension radiating through him. The blown pupils and the way his tongue flicked out to lick his lips let me know it wasn't fear that was racing through him.

As I turned the lock, I moved to press him against the door, trapping him between my body and the rough wood. He didn't protest at my presence or push me away, he just looked up at me with that needy, shocked expression and waited.

"Every man out there is going to know who you belong to, Boy."

Another shiver raced through him, and his hips thrust out to try to grind his cock against mine. His moan was louder that time, and he was so aroused I could feel his hard length even through the layers of loose clothing.

"Who do you belong to?"

There was no doubt on his face, and no hesitation in his voice. "You."

"Sometimes you'll call me your lover...sometimes you'll call me your boyfriend...but not tonight." The last bits of nervous energy faded at my words, and I could almost see the way his desire flared.

"Who am I tonight?" The answer was written on his face, and he didn't even pause before the answer came whispering out.

"Master."

"If something gets too much, you're going to tell me 'red.' 'No' or 'stop' won't work. Do you understand that?" Most people, no matter how little they knew about the lifestyle, would understand what I meant. Thankfully, Randall nodded.

"Safeword."

"Yes." I leaned in and gave him a kiss. "You're going to be a good boy and take your punishment tonight, aren't you? No matter how embarrassed or how turned on you get?"

I got another gaspy breath from him that I thought was a moan he'd tried to hide. His nod was jerkier than it had been before, but he seemed to understand that I was going to push him even further than I had last time.

"Yes…Master." That needy, low voice was hot as fuck.

"Good boy. Let's get you ready, or you're going to be late for work." I'd already warned Jake that I was going to make his server crazy. He'd just shaken his head and mumbled that Andrew was going to drive him insane.

I stepped away, and with only the barest hesitation, Randall started stripping off his shirt. I moved to the corner and sat down on the chair, setting my bag on the floor. He didn't question what was in it. He was either too nervous or too overwhelmed with the options, but either way, I wasn't ready to tell him yet. I leaned back and made no attempt to hide my excitement at watching my boy get naked. He blushed and squirmed, but it was with desire, not fear.

His smooth, muscled body begged for my touch, but I held myself back. I'd have plenty of time to explore my boy later. There was another miniscule hesitation when he reached for the button on his jeans, but before I could even remind him of his safeword, the pants were falling to the floor.

Toeing off his shoes as he looked at me, he stepped out of the pants and just waited. "Very good, Angel. Come here."

His body swayed with that natural grace that only got sexier the more turned on he became. His cock strained against the fabric of his tight briefs, and I knew he was so hard he had to feel trapped. I let my hands reach out to rest on his hips, and I felt a shiver run through him.

My needy boy.

Randall let out a little whimper as I eased his tight underwear over his straining erection. He was so hard, his cock stretched out in front of his body, begging for attention. It was going to have to wait, though. As his briefs fell to the floor, I reached into the small bag at my feet.

I don't know what he was expecting, but the confusion on his face was so cute I almost smiled. It only took seconds for his brain to connect the dots, but it was worth the wait to see his eyes get big and his mouth drop open. And this was the easy part.

"We're going to make sure you stay nice and hard. And it's going to make sure you can't come until I let you, Boy." As I brought the cock ring up to his body, he watched in silence.

I'd chosen a leather one that was incredibly soft but would be completely obvious under his clothing. He didn't want to hide his erection at work, and I didn't want to hide my claim on his body. So it was a win for both of us.

Wrapping the strap around his erection, I carefully tightened it. Just from the look on his face, it was clear he'd never worn one. And the idea that I would be the first to show him had my own need soaring. I was still having a hard time wrapping my mind around the fact that I was his first everything…but I couldn't deny how incredible that made me feel. His trust in me was touching.

"You look beautiful like this, Angel. Every man out there is going to see your trapped cock and know you've given control over it to me. What do you think?" If he was going to call it off, it would be right at that moment. Once he went out and saw how the men would watch him and leer, he'd love it.

With just me and his imagination, I wasn't sure how he would feel. He'd questioned his needs and desires for so long, I wasn't sure if he was ready to take them to the next level. Just getting a job at the bar was a huge step for my dirty angel, but this would seem even bigger.

He took in a shaky breath and his head came up to look at me. "It's…it's okay…that I…and you…"

Tender and sweet would work, but I knew naughty and

straight to the point would get through clearer. I reached out and grabbed his cock with a rough jerk that made his toes curl and his eyes roll back in his head. If it hadn't been for the cock ring, I think he would have come right then. "I'm going to love seeing every man watch you and having them know that you belong to me. I'm going to love seeing you wiggle that ass as you bend over, and watching you grind that cock against the table, knowing you can't come until I let you. You're going to be begging me to come by the end of the night, and you won't care at all who's watching you. I'm going to love every dirty minute of it."

I eased up on the rough handling of his dick and started calming him back down with long, smooth strokes that were too gentle to get him off. "And then I'm going to take you home and hold you and make love to you, if that's what you want. Because you're my boy, and I'm going to give you everything that you need."

Randall was panting and fighting to think as I slowly stopped playing with his cock until I was finally just holding it. Like it was a toy I wasn't ready to release yet. "Do you understand, Angel? Dirty or innocent, or in your case, both... You're still my angel."

His nod was hesitant, but I could see the confidence building in him again as he worked things out in his head. I could almost see his brain whirling, but I knew he would be fine once he got out there and stopped thinking so much. "I understand...Master."

"Good boy." I gave his dick another long stroke as a reward. "Remember," I ran my thumb over the sensitive head, "If you behave, I'll have a reward waiting for you."

He let out a needy, shaky moan and nodded. "I'll... be...I'll...good..."

It was going to be a long night for my dirty angel...and I was going to make it even longer.

"I'm so proud of you. I know you're going to try hard for me. You want to please your master, don't you?" Randall could see the words were leading him somewhere, but he wasn't sure where, and he didn't know what to think.

He gave me another hesitant nod. "I...you've already...and I want..." Randall took a long, slow breath and closed his eyes. "You make it impossible to think when you look at me like that."

My wicked laugh didn't seem to help his concentration any. "Hudson...you have to stop doing that so I can think."

"Why would I want you to do that when you react so beautifully?" My possessive hold on his dick loosened, and I went back to teasing his erection. "All that need and desire... you're the most incredible little thing to watch."

"God, you say...Master...please..."

Since he asked so sweetly, I let his cock just rest in my hand, and he relaxed, trying to find his words. "I want to please you, Master. But it's...the idea of going out there...it's okay if it's hot, right?"

"Yes, Angel. I want to see you so turned on out there that you can't function, and I want you to remember that I chose this as your punishment because it was what I wanted to see. You can't worry about what I'll think if it's my idea." As long as I could keep that in the front of his mind until we went out to the bar, he'd be fine.

He nodded more decisively, eyes still closed in concentration, and I knew similar words had been rolling through his mind all afternoon, probably longer, knowing him. "You're in charge."

"That's right. And all you have to do is obey what I say. Unless you use your safeword, everything is up to me." For some people, that loss of control would make them crazy, but for Randall, it made him feel safe. I couldn't be angry or disgusted if what we were doing was my idea, and he was under my control.

"Yes, Master." God, those were the most beautiful words.

"We're almost done. You're going to have to apologize to Jake for being late, naughty boy." A little shiver ran through him, and he bit down on his lip. Oh yes, the idea of having to grovel and tell Jake how sorry he was sent him into orbit. My dirty angel.

I reached into the bag and pulled out the last two items. "Now turn around and bend over. Show me that sexy ass of yours."

His eyes popped open like I'd said there was a snake in the room. "What?"

I let the little toy rest in the palm of my hand. "I've got one more thing to add to your punishment, naughty boy."

A drop of precum hit the floor as he stared, mouth open, just watching. He was shocked but aroused. He knew what it was. I let the words come out low and full of heat. "Have you ever used a plug, Boy?"

He shook his head, but then stopped and nodded. Hmm. "Is that a yes or no?"

Randall's mouth opened and closed several times before the words came out. "I haven't used a plug, but I have…I have a…a toy at home."

"Does it slide in your tight ass while you imagine getting fucked?" The rough words made his cock jerk in my hand, and he groaned.

"Yes."

"Very good. Then this little thing won't hurt a bit. You know it's going to feel good sliding in, don't you?" My own cock was just as hard as Randall's, and the only thing that kept my brain working was the anticipation of what was to come.

I gave his cock a pat, which made him blush. "Turn around,

then, and reach down to grab your ankles. I want to see that tight little hole."

It was another too-close moment for my boy. Without the cock ring, he would have exploded. Something about the pat or slightly condescending tone did it for him. Eyes still closed, he slowly turned until his full, round ass was facing toward me.

"Good boy." Another shiver raced through him as he bent over and spread his legs. He knew exactly what I wanted to see. It was like he'd imagined this scene a thousand times in his head.

Opening the lube, I tried to make sure he knew what I was doing. I didn't want anything to scare him or make him too nervous. The unknown could be sexy, but in this case, his own imagination would help fuel the fire.

"Some plugs are designed to fit flush to your body so no one would know. I could take you out to dinner or to the movies, and we would be the only people who knew what was inside you, driving you crazy. This one is different." When the toy was ready, I reached out and started teasing the pink skin around his tight pucker.

Not entering him yet…just making the need build.

"This one has a long base that is going to show every time you move. When you walk, they're going to see the toy just enough to make them watch your ass. When you bend over, they're going to see the base sticking out of your tight little body." He moaned as I let one finger slide into his hole.

There was no resistance, no fear about how it would feel. My boy had definitely been playing with his toy, but he was still hot and tight, so I knew he'd feel every inch of the plug. It wasn't wide, but it would sit deep enough inside him that it would brush up against his prostate if he found the right angle. Walking would work fine, but I was betting that when he leaned over, it would be like fireworks going off inside him.

The fact that it had a little remote was going to help that feeling along.

Another groan ripped out of him as I sank my finger in deep. He started thrusting back, almost without thought, wanting more. Two fingers made him pause, but the stretch had him gasping, and I could see his grip on his ankles getting even tighter.

"You want to touch your cock, don't you? Feeling my fingers fuck you makes you just want to come." It was so easy to make him fly; he was incredible.

His head jerked up and down, and he moaned. "Please…"

"Not yet. You have to be punished. You came without permission, remember?"

He nodded reluctantly, and his face tightened as he tried to do what he was told.

"I was naughty."

"And naughty boys have to be punished." I eased my fingers out and brought the toy up to his ass before he could finish his protest. Someone didn't want to be empty. The smooth black toy had a tapered head that went in easily. If he'd never played with his ass before it might have been more difficult for him, but his body pulled it right in.

My wicked angel liked playing with his ass.

And I would be a terrible master if I didn't make sure to give him everything that he craved.

The base of the plug stuck out about an inch or so away from his body. It would give me something to hold on to, and it would give the men a show they wouldn't forget. By the time it was fully seated, Randall was panting, and his muscles were clenched.

I gave it a pat, and he moaned so loudly I knew they heard it out front. "Alright, let's get you dressed. Show me how that uniform looks, Angel."

He slowly straightened and had to take several shaky

breaths before he could make his body work. Jake was going to kill me. His server would be nearly useless tonight, but I didn't think the men were going to mind. The little gasps of pleasure and deep moans that echoed through the room as Randall got dressed assured that.

By the time he got his clothes on—his tight, nearly painted-on jeans and shirt—he'd gotten himself under control, but it was a fight he wouldn't be able to win. I was going to make sure of that.

12

RANDALL

PEOPLE DIDN'T REALLY SPONTANEOUSLY combust, did they?

Answering that question would have been easier if I could've made my brain work. But just walking from the back room to the bar took more effort than I ever would have thought possible, so every brain cell was focused on that.

The light touch Hudson kept on my back as we walked out into the room didn't help, either. I kept imagining his hand moving lower and wiggling the toy. Cock ring or not, I knew if he just teased it a little more, I would get to come.

It was maddening. And every eye in the room was on me, only making it worse. Their hot gazes followed me as I tried to stay focused on Jake, but all I wanted to do was rub up against Hudson and come. It had been days since I'd orgasmed, and now it felt like it was right in front of me, but just out of my reach.

I let out a little whimper as I leaned against the bar. Standing up straight wasn't so bad...or maybe wasn't as good... but leaning over pressed the tip of the plug into my prostate and sent lightning up my spine.

The low hum of voices finally picked up. The silence had been deafening, but knowing they were talking about me made me feel even more wicked. I just had to keep reminding myself that it was what Hudson wanted. It might have been stupid, but that made it easier.

It seemed giving up that control meant giving up the fears and worries.

I'd never felt so free...or so horny.

When he'd taken out the cock ring, my mind had gone completely blank. Then every naughty thing I'd ever seen with them online had started flashing through my mind. The plug had been the icing on what would be a very dirty cake. It was more than I'd ever dreamed of. And it was all his idea.

Him flirting with me at the bar was one thing, but this was another.

Jake finally finished up with a customer and walked over to the end of the bar where I was waiting. "You ready for work? I'm not paying you to get off in the back."

The words were rough, but the laughter and heat in his eyes said he wasn't mad...just turned on.

He'd gotten turned on by me.

Fuck.

"I'm sorry I'm late...I...Hudson..." Hudson's hand moved down and gave my ass a pat. It felt like a reminder to behave, and to follow his orders. "Master had to punish me."

I was going to combust right there.

Flames were shooting through every nerve in me, and all I wanted to do was whimper and beg Hudson to take me and let me come. The rational part of me knew this wasn't supposed to be hot, but it was. It was perfect. The humiliation and the embarrassment just made the need stronger.

"We heard." Jake's words were deep and low, but Andrew just leaned against the bar and nodded, fanning himself dramatically.

"God, did we ever." Andrew gave me a look like he'd gladly eat me up, and Jake just growled.

"Go grab your tray. You've got customers waiting." Jake's demanding words made me start to move, but Hudson did something to the plug and it started vibrating. Every thought flew out of my head.

It was insane. All I could do was hold on to the bar and ride out the pleasure. As I arched up, my cock rubbed against the smooth wood of the bar, and it made everything even crazier. The pleasure fired through every nerve and bounced around like the little ball in those arcade games that just kept lighting things up.

When he finally stopped, I got a pat on the ass. It was embarrassing and perfection all in one. Hudson's deep voice made me want to roll over and plead for his touch. "Go on, Randy…people are waiting."

Randy? He never called me that.

The question must have shown on my face because he chuckled low, and the sound went right to my hard cock. "Randall might be my little twink who shakes his ass at the customers, but Randy is the little slut who grinds his bound cock on the bar and begs to come."

I had?

Fuck.

Nodding, because I really couldn't complain, I took a deep breath and picked up the tray. Looking out at the sea of devilish grins and napkins all over the floor, I had to groan. It was going to be a long night.

I WAS RIGHT. ONLY TWO HOURS INTO MY SHIFT AND I WAS ready to climb the walls…or hump them…that sounded reasonable too.

Hudson was good about letting me carry the drinks without hitting his magic button, but when my hands were empty or I was leaning over the table, all bets seemed to be off. My cock was so hard it ached, and with the toy wrapped around it, no matter what I did, I knew I wasn't going to come.

As I walked up to the bar, I saw Hudson in his favorite corner, leaning against the wall. He just watched me with his fiery gaze never leaving me. Maybe some people would have felt stalked, or even claustrophobic, but I loved knowing he was completely focused on me.

Setting my tray down, I handed Jake the money and receipts I'd collected from the men and braced myself. But the buzzing pleasure didn't come. Looking over at Hudson, I saw him crooking that finger at me, calling me over. I really was his boy, because it never even occurred to me to question or push back...I just went to him.

He spread his legs, and I settled between them, desperately hoping he would do something to help ease the need. One of his arms wrapped around me, and his hand settled on my ass, temptingly close to the plug I knew everyone was staring at.

Just the images dancing around in my head made it hard to think.

"How is my little slut doing?" His fingers nudged the plug, and I moaned, arching into his hand. "Is my little Randy needy?"

"Yes...Master...I..."

"You were naughty, weren't you? That's why you have to be punished." Dirty catcalls echoed through the room, and I knew I was blushing, but my cock just got harder if that was even possible.

"I was naughty...but I've been good." I'd been so good.

His free hand moved to cup my crotch, and his fingers teased over my hard dick. "You're taking your punishment very well. It's not over, though. You're nowhere near desperate enough."

Could you die from being so turned on that your body just shattered?

I couldn't even think. "But…"

His smile was wicked, and it only made the men more excited. Jake kept mumbling about the chaos, but I think he'd sold more beer in one night than he had the rest of the week combined. Even if it was just to get me to go pick up the empty bottles.

Hudson's teasing fingers pinched my dick, and he moved the plug again. There was no way to hide how incredible it felt, even if I'd wanted to. But I didn't. I liked knowing they could tell just how turned on I was. And having them know it was Hudson that was in control was the hottest thing ever.

Even my dirtiest fantasies couldn't have lived up to the reality.

"Back to work." Jake's voice broke through the pleasure, but the embarrassment of knowing he was watching just made it harder to think. "Fuck him on your time. Not mine."

Dead. I was dead. Spontaneous human combustion.

"Oh, I will." Hudson gave my ass another swat. Harder, making my breath catch in my throat. "You liked that, didn't you, little slut?"

Denying it would be stupid when the way my body shook and the moan that escaped showed just how much I liked it. Hudson laughed, wicked and low, and pulled me close. Whispering in my ear, only for me, he murmured, "I'm going to make love to you tonight and send you flying, but one day, I'm going to bend you over and give you the spanking I know you're desperate for."

The men called out desperate pleas to know what Hudson was saying. He just gave them a wink and ignored the curious questions. Was it weird that the words were almost sweet?

Tender? They probably shouldn't have been, but the way he said it made me warm inside.

He knew who I really was, and it didn't matter to him. It made him want me more...and not because I was a little slut who was fun to tease...he just wanted me. No matter who I was at that moment.

"Please."

"One day, little slut." His hand came down again, and that time I knew it was to tease the men, so it made it even more erotic. "Now go back to work."

"Yes, Master." That was never going to get old.

I could still feel his hand on my ass even after I'd gone halfway across the room. It'd been careful and light, there probably wasn't even a mark, but he'd *spanked* me. The way he'd talked about bending me over his lap made me lightheaded. No one had ever said anything like that to me.

The guys must have *loved* it, because there were almost a dozen napkins and odd pieces of silverware on the floor. I wasn't sure where they'd gotten all the spoons from, but I'd had to have picked up at least ten already.

Cleaning up the trash and other objects from the floor was like walking through a minefield of sexual tension. Every time I bent over, not only did the plug rub against my prostate, but Hudson would hit the remote, and I had to fight not to plead for more.

It'd felt like I'd come close to orgasming a thousand times, but it was never close enough. It was always just out of reach. By the time I'd reached the fourth piece, holding in the moans was impossible. By the seventh, I didn't even care how loud I was. By the last napkin, I was shaking and working the plug as I bent over. I knew the men closest to me were probably getting a hell of a show, but I just couldn't help it.

If there had been a chance to calm down and catch my breath, it wouldn't have been so hard...but then it probably wouldn't have been so incredible, either. Relaxing would have meant thinking, and that would have sent me down a path of self-doubt and second-guessing.

I didn't want that. I wanted to give in to Hudson without worrying and without questioning.

There were no requests for another round or even any questions. They all just watched as I walked over to that far table where the bottles were lined up neatly in rows, clearly waiting for me. I probably should have asked for a break, curled up in Hudson's arms for a moment. It just didn't occur to me.

And endless pleasure as a punishment was the most incredible way to remind me who was in charge.

As I leaned over the table, my cock ran along the hard edge, sending sparks up my spine. It felt like I'd been hard for days, not just hours. Every caress of my jeans was almost too much. Every time Hudson ran his fingers carefully over my erection, it made me want to beg.

It was finally just too much.

Thrusting my cock against the table, I let the pleasure build, determined to make it enough. Between the cock ring and the plug, I knew I was almost there. I gave up pretending to pick up the empty bottles and just chased the need growing inside me.

I was either going to come or explode. At that moment, it didn't matter which.

Strong arms wrapped around me, and Hudson pulled me back against his body. "Who do you belong to, Angel?"

"You!"

"Who controls your pleasure?"

"You." It came out needier and desperate. "Please."

"Have you learned your lesson? I'm not sure you have." His voice dropped low, and I closed my eyes, soaking up the feel of his body pressed against mine and the words as they flowed through me. "Humping the table when you knew you had to wait. I'm not sure you learned your lesson."

"I'm sorry. I learned my lesson." If he'd asked, I couldn't have told him what rule I'd broken, or why I was being punished; everything was just focused on the fire that wouldn't die.

"We'll talk about that, but I think my boy needs to come. Are you ready?" His breath was hot against my skin as he whispered in my ear.

A less trusting person would have asked "ready for what," but it didn't even occur to me. All I knew was that the wait was finally over, and I was going to get to come. "Yes! Please, Master."

I felt the world spin around me as Hudson turned me in his arms. His hands came down and gripped my ass, pulling me up so I could wrap myself around him. My cock rubbed against his firm abs, and the rough pleasure made me moan again.

He started to move, and I pressed my face against his neck. I should have insisted I walk. But the feel of his hands on my ass, nudging the plug with every step, and the way I got to writhe on him, fucking my cock against his body, was too good to push away. I didn't even care who saw me or how I looked.

I was going to get to come. That was all that mattered.

We didn't even make it to the employee's bathroom.

One moment we were walking, and the next, I was pressed against the wall and he was taking my mouth. It was hot and wet and perfect—but it wasn't enough. I kept trying to rub my cock against him or move the plug deeper, but my orgasm was still out of reach.

When he pulled away, I opened my eyes. Before I could find the words to beg him for more, he was lowering me to the ground. When he saw I was steady enough to stand, he started lowering himself to his knees.

It took me entirely too long to understand what was going to happen. In my defense, I was a virgin, and he'd fried my brain at least an hour before, so I didn't feel too bad about it.

He was so tall and broad that he still looked huge kneeling there in front of me. His position should have implied submission or releasing control, but I knew who was still in charge. The wait was impossibly long, even though it only took seconds for him to release the button on my pants and ease the zipper over my cock.

"I told you if you were good you'd get a reward."

Hudson didn't take the restraint off my cock. He just swallowed me down in one smooth motion until I could feel my cock hitting the back of his throat and sliding into the tight heat. Fuck. I whimpered as he came back up and I lost the perfect pleasure. But it only took seconds until his mouth wrapped around me again.

No gagging. No effort. He just took me deep into his mouth and tried to suck my brains out through my cock. He succeeded.

I knew I was loud, but there was no way to hold back the whimpers or the moans. Shouts of pleasure burst out as his throat teased at the head of my cock. It was the most incredible thing ever. I'd thought that nothing could have felt as good as the things we'd already done, but I was wrong.

Very wrong.

When the frantic need began to build again, and I could feel my orgasm start racing through me, I started to panic. I was afraid I'd lose it like I had the other times I'd been so close, but Hudson was there. Master wasn't going to let it go again.

The pleasure built and swelled inside of me like a balloon ready to burst, shattering into a million pieces. Just when I knew it couldn't get any bigger, Hudson started making the plug vibrate again, and the crazy need started to grow even bigger.

I'd thought the tortuous pleasure couldn't get worse, but

when he started the plug again, I knew he'd just been teasing me before. It was like lightning shooting straight up through me. The vibration was so strong it was almost painful.

Before I could even decide how it felt, Hudson swallowed my cock deep, and his hand moved between my legs to play with the toy. The combination was too much.

I shattered.

His strong grip held me as I shook, and the orgasm blasted its way out of me. I'd never felt anything like it. Every climax I'd ever had was like a pale imitation of what he could do to me. As the pleasure faded and I sagged against the wall, I fought to keep my eyes open.

Part of me wanted to curl up in his arms and sleep, but the fact that my cock was still achingly hard and he was still teasing it with his mouth made that impossible. It was so sensitive I thought about trying to pull away, but my cock was still begging to come. The conflicting signals were maddening.

Hudson saw the struggle, but didn't let up on the pleasure. We both knew I had my safeword, but something about squirming and writhing while he kept up the incredible sensations felt perfect and wicked. When it was almost too much, he released my cock but moved his hands to roll my full balls between his fingers.

"I came, but it feels like I didn't." The words were husky and rough, almost like I was starting to lose my voice.

His grin was wicked, and he leaned in and flicked his tongue over my red, sensitive dick. "I know. And you're going to stay that way until I let you come again."

I wasn't sure if that was a threat or a promise, but it sent shivers racing through me. "Again?"

"I'm not done with you yet. Remember? I promised to make love to you all night." Desire flashed through his eyes, and a little whimper escaped me as I imagined what that might mean. I had a feeling it was going to be a long time before he let me come again. I should have probably had my head examined, but the idea of him unleashing all that pleasure on me again was perfect.

Hudson…Master…boyfriend…Dominant…I was ready to make love to the man who held me so tenderly and pushed me right to the edge.

13

HUDSON

THERE WAS passion in his eyes, and he moved so beautifully when I played with his cock, but he couldn't seem to get his hands working enough to pull his pants back up. I knew Jake would keep people away from the back as long as he could, but eventually, someone would need to use one of the customer restrooms, or Jake would need something from the storeroom.

Having Randall show off that beautiful trapped cock through his pants was one thing, naked was another. At least until we had a few more long discussions.

"Let me help you, Angel. I've got it." Easing Randall's hands away from his tight pants, I started working them up his thighs and tucking his dick back in. "Are you ready to go home to my place?"

Randall's head fell back, and he moaned as I rubbed my fingers over the head of his cock. He was still so hard and sensitive, I knew the sensations had to feel incredible. There was a sleepiness to him that made me want to wrap my arms around him, but he wouldn't be able to relax until he'd come again and that ring was off his dick.

We'd talked about the punishment possibilities and plans for the night. I knew what Randall wanted, but the idea that I was going to be the first person he made love with was daunting. I didn't think I'd ever been anybody's first.

It wasn't the whole taking his virginity thing, because that mentality was stupid. It was just…special, I guess, that he was taking that step with me. And I had to admit, the caveman inside me liked the idea that he would always remember this night.

His legs seemed moderately steadier as I finished buttoning his pants, so I gave him a kiss and stepped back. "I'm going to grab your bag. Don't move."

His hands started inching away from the wall. "And *don't* touch your cock."

His eyes opened, and they looked slightly unfocused, with his pupils wide. "But—"

Randall still looked so needy and desperate. "I'll let you play with it. But there'll be consequences later. Because that cock belongs to me, doesn't it?"

"More *punishments*?" The word was filled with breathless anticipation, and I had to fight not to smile.

"No, just consequences for playing with something that belongs to your master." That earned me another breathy little moan, but he nodded and reached down to start running his fingers over his erection.

Hurry. I had to hurry, or we'd never make it out of the bar.

His first time was *not* going to be in the employee bathroom.

Gathering up our stuff only took seconds, but in the short amount of time I'd been gone, he'd moved his other hand between his legs. I knew he was playing with the plug, and just the image of him stretched out on my bed, naked and teasing himself with the toy, made my dick even harder.

He had to be trying to kill me.

"Did I say you got to play with the plug? Is my dirty angel teasing his tight little hole?" I crowded against Randall. He blinked up at me, confused, but didn't let go of his toys. Either of them.

"But it's...and they're..." His voice broke and he started to shake.

"No playing with the plug, Boy. You don't get to come again right now." His lower lip pouted out, and his hand started working the plug even faster.

Naughty boy.

"I'm so close..." His eyes closed again, and the hand on his cock started teasing it in short, fast strokes.

Pulling his hands away from his body, I pinned them to the wall. God, he was incredible. He was also mine and needed to remember that. "Who do you belong to, Angel?"

Those beautiful, sexy eyes opened. "You."

"Who does this cock belong to?" I let one leg push against his dick, and it made him gasp.

"You." Need filled the word.

"That was very naughty, Boy. Tell me what you did wrong." I knew the words echoed down the hallway, because all the noise in the bar stopped again. Some part of Randall must have realized it as well, because his eyes flickered toward the front of the building, and he gave a small moan.

My little exhibitionist.

"I touched myself when you said to stop." He bit his lip, and gave me a pleading look. "I'm sorry. I was bad. Do you have to punish me?"

So fuckin' perfect.

"Naughty boys who disobey their master have to be punished, don't they?" There was only one thing I knew was on his mind. Had my little slut disobeyed just to get spanked? If so, he was definitely becoming more comfortable with what he needed.

"Yes, Master." The low, sexy words were met with absolute

silence, and I knew every man in there was hanging on his needy words.

I set the bags on the ground and roughly turned Randall to face the wall. There was a sharp inhale when I surprised him, but a groan when he realized he was getting exactly what he wanted. "You're going to remember this, Angel. You're going to remember what happens to naughty boys."

He was shaking, and his fingers were sliding down the wall, desperate for something to hold on to, by the time I had the pants pulled down again. His cock was stuck in his jeans, but that only made him look hotter and feel dirtier. This wasn't about his trapped hard-on or even getting to come.

This was about submitting and letting every man out there hear what a dirty little slut he was.

I leaned close and whispered just for him as I brought my hand down the first time. "You're going to look so beautiful wearing my marks on your ass."

The strangled gasp turned into a sharp cry of shock as my hand met his skin, and the smack carried down the hall. The rumble of voices in the bar let us both hear that the men knew exactly what was happening.

Randall's head went down to rest on the wall, but he pushed his butt out, giving me a needy whimper. I brought my hand down again on his other cheek, loving the way his ass quivered and seemed desperate for more. I wasn't spanking him hard, but his skin was already starting to pink. He was incredible.

I let another smack fall on his ass, and then gave the cheek a rough squeeze. Randall moaned, and his hips started to move like he was fucking the air. The sharp sting only seemed to make his desire stronger. Bringing my hand down again, his cry of pain and pleasure made my cock ache, and I knew every man listening would be in the same situation. But this sweet, perfect boy was mine.

"My dirty angel. I know how much you need, and I can't

wait to give you everything." I kneaded his cheeks and listened to his whimpers and pleas for more. "It's time to go home. So I can fill up this tight little body and make you fly."

"Please...Master...Hudson...please...I..." He was so close to the edge, but I wasn't going to let him fall. Not yet, at least.

Pulling up his pants was even harder the second time. All I wanted to do was strip him down, not get him dressed again. Once he was ready, some of the fog had started to clear, but desire was still raging through him. He leaned into me and sighed, holding me tight. "When we get back to your house? No more waiting?"

"That's right, Angel." I wrapped my arms around him, careful not to hit him with the bags. "I'm going to kiss you and lick—"

"Hudson!" He gasped out the word and poked me with his finger. "You can't do that to me."

Laughing quietly, I leaned down and kissed the top of his head. "Oh, but I can. I'm going to describe every detail to you as we head home."

"More punishments?" Then he giggled, making him look even more innocent but completely debauched.

"No, just because I love making you crazy." Randall straightened and shook his head, smiling. The need was still there, like a deep current that I could feel swirling around him, but he looked steadier, and less like I'd just fucked him in the hallway.

Wrapping one arm around him, I started leading him to the front of the building. I'd parked just down the street, so we didn't have far to go, but I knew with the plug, it was going to feel like a lot longer.

My teasing and touches probably wouldn't help, either, but that didn't mean I was going to stop.

The natural movement of the plug as he walked, and my wandering fingers, had him letting out low moans by the time we started through the sea of men. There was no reason to hide what we'd done, because they'd heard every smack and plea, so I just kept teasing the plug and kneading his ass as we headed out.

Catcalls and dirty jokes were called out, but Randall just blushed and squirmed. Andrew was leaning on the bar, watching with a heated look that Jake didn't miss. As we walked out the door, Jake had Andrew wrapped in his arms and was taking his mouth in a demanding kiss that had everyone's attention.

The drive home went too fast for me, but too slow for Randall.

I kept him squirming and moaning as I touched and teased him at stoplights and then told him all the ways I was going to kiss and taste him when we finally got home. The base of the plug pushed against the seat, only making it harder for him to think. By the time I finally parked, he was pleading, and I knew the collar around his dick was the only reason his pants weren't soaked with precum.

We got into the house in record time, but once the door closed, things slowed down considerably. Kissing and stripping off his clothes, we worked our way through the small condo, finally making it to the bedroom when he was naked and begging.

The fact that I still had clothes on only seemed to make him more turned on. I hadn't done it on purpose. I'd just been focused on him, not me. I was going to take my time exploring his delectable body, and for that, he had to be naked.

Randall let out a low gasp of surprise as I picked him up and carried him over to the bed. Stretching out over him, I pinned his hands above his head and looked down his lean body. Muscles quivered and his cock stuck out obscenely, red and begging for attention.

"Hold on to the headboard, and don't let go." Randall had

been too turned on for too long to question anything. He reached out, frantically trying to obey. The drive for more was the only thing on his mind.

Finally having him all to myself, I took a moment to simply gaze at him. I propped up on one elbow and used my free hand to trail my fingers down his arm. He squirmed and spread his legs, silently begging for me to move lower. But I wasn't ready for that yet. There was so much of my boy I hadn't explored.

I might have teased and touched, but he'd never been spread out and begging for me. I leaned down and gave him a slow, tender kiss. Keeping it light and gentle, I tried to pour what I was feeling into him. I wasn't sure exactly where we stood beyond the understanding that he belonged to me in the bedroom, but I knew we were much more than just lovers or a Dom and his submissive.

Releasing his mouth, I kissed down his jaw and neck, working my way to the little pebbled nipples that called to me. I ran my tongue around the stiff peaks and listened to the desperate noises that escaped my boy.

"What do you think, Angel? Do you want my mouth on them?" Randall shivered and cried out for my touch.

I gave him a wicked grin. "They seem so sensitive. Should I lick them, or do you think they want something sharper? Something just a bit rougher than that?"

His mouth opened and closed, and he couldn't seem to decide what to say. Theory only went so far, and I knew he must have played with his nipples before, but having someone else's hands on his body was completely different.

"Are you usually gentle, or do you play with them mercilessly? Do you make them hurt?" From the look on his face, I already knew the answer.

He was so desperate, the words jumped out of him. "Hurt. It feels so good when they hurt."

My needy little pain slut.

"I'm going to make them hurt so good, Angel." He gasped out as my lips wrapped around one nipple, and I used my teeth to tug on the tender bud.

There was no reason to go slow. We'd teased and passed the foreplay stage hours ago. In that moment, all my boy wanted was to be taken and to come. I nibbled and licked until his nipples were puffy and red and he was crying out in pleasure. His hips kept thrusting up, trying to get my touch, but I wasn't ready yet.

When they were tender, and so sensitive I knew he'd feel them every time his shirt brushed against them the next day, I started kissing down his chest and abs. He couldn't seem to decide if he was relieved I'd moved on or ready for more attention to his nipples, because he kept looking down at me and then back to them, licking his lips and squirming.

"I think those need to be pierced. Should I take you down and have them put little rings in them for me to touch and tug on?" I licked around his belly button and smiled as he squirmed, his eyes getting wider as I described what I wanted to do to him. "Everyone at the bar would be able to see them through your shirt. I could wrap my arms around you and play with them while everyone watched. I might even be able to make you come just by tugging on them."

Randall simply stared, his mouth hanging open and a shocked look on his face. But he didn't tell me no. Had he considered them before? He had to have seen them in porn or in pictures. "Have you thought about getting those little nubs pierced, Angel?"

Embarrassment flashed across his face, and his cock jerked. His words came out breathy and low. "Yes, but people don't…they…"

"Oh, but they do, and you're going to look so sexy. I'll take you down to the shop, strip off your shirt, and show them just where I want you pierced. They'll know who you belong to,

Boy." That seemed to thrill him just as much as getting the actual nipple rings did. His red, hard cock jerked again, and a drop of precum leaked out the top to bead at the tip of his dick.

As I pushed his legs apart and moved to lie between them, I licked the drip and watched him writhe. "You liked your reward earlier, didn't you?"

Randall moaned and frantically nodded. "Yes...please..."

"You want more? You want my mouth wrapped around your cock?" Hearing him beg was better than guessing or even knowing what he wanted.

"Yes...it was...and please...yes..." Full sentences were impossible, but he was still holding on to the headboard and doing his best to behave, so I wanted to reward my good boy.

"I like sucking on your dick and making you squirm and beg, but I have something even better for my boy." He might have been too wound up to talk, but he knew what was coming when I spread his legs even wider and opened him up completely to my gaze.

Lowering my head, I stretched out between his legs and pushed them up to his chest. The need and anticipation mixed with the embarrassment of being vulnerable, and it kicked his desire even higher.

"You are incredible, Angel." I kissed the inside of his thigh. "So sexy and so beautiful."

I touched my lips to his other leg, slowly working toward his plugged opening. "Watching you bend over for me earlier was perfect. That ass," another kiss even closer, "And that tight little hole just begging to be filled even more."

Randall let out a strangled scream as my tongue finally flicked out and ringed the sensitive skin around the plug. I moved my hand up and pulled the plug out to its widest point, then eased it back in again. He thrust his hips back, trying for more, and I felt hands threading their way through my hair.

"Naughty boy." I gave the plug a tap, and he cried out, moving his hands back to the rails.

"I'm sorry, Hudson!"

Wanting him to know it was alright, I pulled the plug all the way out, then started fucking him slowly with the toy. "Next time you disobey, I'll have to punish you, Angel."

The threat of another spanking, or something even better, had him shaking and his cock leaking even more. The ring made it hard for cum to escape the tight restraint, so to see it dripping down his dick, I knew his desire was at a feverish level.

"Do you want my mouth on your pretty hole?" The dirty words pushed him even higher. Things tumbled out of his lips that didn't make any sense, he just wanted more.

Tossing the plug aside, I lapped at his tight hole and fucked it with my fingers, stretching him even more and making sure he was ready. One day, I was going to feast on his tempting ass and see if I could make him come just by eating him out, but he was too desperate to draw it out any longer.

When I pulled away to find the condom and lube in my nightstand, he cried out, "No, please, I'll be good."

Stretching over him, I gave him a tender kiss. His surprise as he tasted my lips made me smile. "Are you ready for more, Angel? We don't have to go any further if you don't want to. I'll make you come and kiss you all night, but if you're not ready to make love, that's okay."

He shook his head and his arms came down to wrap around me. "I need you. I'm ready. No one has ever...nothing...you don't think I'm wrong or..." The words tumbled out, getting jumbled in his emotions, but I knew what he was trying to say.

"You are perfect just the way you are." I kissed his forehead. "You're sweet and smart and naughty." I kissed his nose, which made him smile. "Perfect for me. I wouldn't have you any other way, my dirty angel."

"Make love to me." Simple words but full of meaning.

The lube and condom took only seconds. All my thoughts of making love to him slowly and tenderly flew out the window as he clung to me and writhed, thrusting his hips up as I stretched out over him. "Please, I need you, Hudson."

The plug and the teasing had him stretched, so I lined my cock up with his needy hole and slid in slowly. He gasped out, and his body bowed off the bed as I slowly entered him. When my dick caressed over his prostate, he gasped again, and his legs tightened against my sides like he was trying to pull me close and keep me from leaving. But I wasn't going anywhere.

When I was fully seated, I stilled and let him adjust to the feeling. He was more than ready, and I wasn't seeing pain on his face. My wicked angel might have technically been a virgin, but he'd played with his ass enough to know how to relax.

His eyes opened and looked at me in an unfocused haze. I wasn't sure if he was actually seeing me, or if he was lost in his own mind. "Hudson." His hips gave a tentative movement, and he cried out. "Please. You have to move. Before I say something stupid."

God, he was so fuckin' cute.

I flexed my hips and slowly pulled out a few inches and then slid deep inside him again. Thinking was hard, but that befuddled desire on his face made me kiss him tenderly. "What do you want to say?"

Randall shook his head, frustration growing in his voice. "Please. You're...Hudson."

Another quick thrust had him moaning, but then I stopped again. I was driving him crazy, but I wanted to know every little thing going through his head. "Tell me what's trying to get out. What do you think is stupid, Angel?"

He blushed, but when I pulled out and nailed his prostate, filling him up again, suddenly it wasn't that important. Telling me just to make me continue fucking him would work and I would get to know what was on my sweet boy's mind. "Tell me."

His fingers were digging into my arms, and I knew I'd have bruises later, but he was shaking so badly he didn't even seem to notice. "You're inside me! And huge! And I sound like a moron, but there…there's so many…please!"

Too much teasing and I was going to fry his brain before he told me everything. Slowly working my hips in tight circles, I tried to keep him on edge but not enough to make him lose his train of thought again. "Tell me, Angel."

Those big, wide eyes blinked up at me in confusion and desire. "I matter, right? I know this is a stupid time to ask, and you're inside me, and everything seems so…but…this is serious for you? And I'm ridiculous and clingy and—"

I took his mouth in a hot, demanding kiss and fucked him sharply, chasing the breath from his body. When I pulled back, he was wearing that same lost expression but a little more worried than before. "Angel, I've never been more serious about anyone. I know the physical side of this is new to you, but everything else is new for me. The insane need to make you mine and keep you close. The way I want to wrap myself around you and never let you go. And I love the way you need me and come to me. I don't want you to change anything. You're my perfect dirty angel."

"You're just…Hudson…" Randall reached up and cupped my face, emotions swirling in his eyes, and pulled me down for another kiss.

I started moving again, wanting to chase the worries and hesitation from his eyes. Everything was too soon and too fast, but I didn't want to slow down. I was racing for more right there beside him. It only took a handful of thrusts before he was gasping out and writhing below me on the bed.

Every thought was gone, and he was just radiating overwhelming need. He was so beautiful I wanted to keep him like that forever, with desire pouring from him. But my boy had been hard and desperate for too long. The orgasm he'd had at the bar hadn't been enough. It had just been the tip of the iceberg.

When his pleas turned to whimpers and he was getting lost in the pleasure, I knew it was time. I didn't want him to sink into subspace, but as he moved, I could see how close he was. Reaching between us, I gave him shallow circles as I released the cock ring.

One thrust was all it took.

I wrapped my fingers around him in a tight, almost punishing grip that sent my little pain slut flying and pegged his prostate in one hard thrust. He screamed out his pleasure, and the desire echoed around the room, loud enough I knew my neighbors heard.

As his body clenched and shook with the force of his orgasm, I finally started chasing mine. A handful of thrusts was all it took, and I was right there with him, flying into the pleasure with him in my arms.

When all that was left was the aftershocks of his desire, and he was looking at me with an almost angelic peace on his face, I curled around him and gave him another innocent kiss. "I've never been more serious, Angel."

I was rapidly falling in love with my sweet boy, and I couldn't think of any reason to fight it.

14

RANDALL

THERE WAS no way I was going to get any studying done. I'd been staring at the same page for almost ten minutes. Part of the problem was that I was starting to care less and less about what I was supposed to be learning. The other piece was that it had been almost three days since I'd seen Hudson, and I was horny.

And a little lonely. But horny sounded better, less needy.

Maybe if the previous weekend hadn't been so incredible, time wouldn't have dragged on so badly. I'd crashed hard after we'd made love the first time. I remembered being curled up in his arms and the feel of his body sliding out of mine, then nothing until the next morning.

There hadn't been time to relax and take it slow because we'd both had places to be, but he'd made me come twice before I'd left his house, once in the shower, wow, and then over the kitchen table. I was never going to be able to look at eggs the same way again.

Before I'd left, he'd made it very clear he'd wanted me back at his house after my classes were over. The rough, demanding look on his face when he'd pinned me to the door and given me the clear orders had my cock stirring even as I remembered it.

The rest of the weekend had been a blur of sex and cuddling together. By Sunday morning, we'd actually gotten out of bed and functioned like a regular couple. I'd tried making breakfast while he'd played games on his phone, pretending to be reading the paper, but that hadn't gone as planned, so we'd headed out to a diner down the street.

By lunch, I'd had to leave because we'd both received calls and texts demanding our presence at different family gatherings, but even my parents hadn't been able to ruin the perfection of that weekend. They'd certainly tried, though.

I'd had to listen to my mother go on and on about the doctor said this and the doctor said that. The guy was either a saint or a serial killer because to her, he was damned near perfect. He sounded so boring I wasn't sure I'd be able to even talk to him at the party, much less try to make a "good impression." It didn't matter that I'd told her repeatedly that I wasn't interested, and that I didn't want to date him. I was evidently just supposed to catch the doctor's eye since I "wasn't getting any younger."

Sometimes I wasn't sure they knew I was a guy. Or what century this was.

"I'm pretty sure no one even says that to women these days, much less a guy."

"What?"

Shit.

I'd been getting too distracted studying in my room, so I'd gone out to the living room for a change of scenery. I'd been alone when I'd sat down but hadn't realized one of my suitemates had wandered in.

"Sorry, talking to myself."

Landon was a little older and had gone back to school to get his MBA. His family ran in the same circles mine did, so I'd done my best to stay under his radar. When we'd first moved into the same suite he'd tried to invite me out for coffee a couple of times, but the idea of how badly it could go once he figured out I was weird had kept me far away from him.

It was amazing how easy it was to avoid someone when you were scared that they would find out your dirty secret.

"That's okay, man. You seem…stressed. Everything okay?" He was a nice guy. He actually seemed concerned and had one of those personalities that radiated confidence and strength without being obnoxious. He probably would have actually listened to all the crazy going through my head, but I knew better than that.

"Just school and parents…" I shrugged, trying to play it off. "Typical stuff."

"Yeah, I get ya." He didn't seem to buy it for even a minute, so I started gathering up my stuff, doing my best to look casual.

No, I'm not running because you're getting nosy. Honest. Nothing to see here. Go back to making lunch and looking sexy.

Who looked hot in baggy sweats and an old T-shirt, anyway?

Landon.

Short dark hair and sculpted features made him look classically handsome, as my mother would say, but his body looked like something I'd seen in porn. The expensive, dirty kind. I didn't even feel bad for noticing. Hudson would have just laughed at me and teased me, and it wasn't like I was planning on hitting on the guy. He was probably straight anyway. I hadn't talked to him enough to know, though. It was just usually a safe bet.

"I'll try to study later. I've got a few errands to run, anyway." And I'd neatly backed myself into a corner. Great. Where could I go? Library? Bookstore? Coffee! "See ya later."

I headed back into my room to drop off my books before he could ask me anything else and was out the door in seconds. Calling out a quick goodbye, I headed down the stairs. The elevator would have made more sense, but I had too much energy to wait, and I wanted to get some distance between me and the guy who could accidentally rat me out to my parents. Paranoid, maybe, but I also could be right.

My nerves probably didn't need coffee, but I had a couple of hours before my first class and it was going to be a long night, so caffeine was probably a good idea, anyway. The shop was at the other end of the campus, so I didn't go over much, but since I wasn't getting anything else done, there was no reason not to enjoy myself.

The walk across the campus helped me relax, but it gave me too much time to think.

First of all, I had to figure out what to do about my mother. Her insistence on introducing me to the doctor guy was going to be embarrassing for all of us once he realized I was taken. Very taken. Hudson wasn't going to share like that, not that I wanted him to. Being watched and teased was very different than dating some boring guy to please my mother.

Was Hudson ready for the chaos that would erupt once my parents knew? Hell, was I ready? I was still getting a degree I didn't really want, just so I didn't have to argue with them and pick something else. She was going to lose her marbles when she realized she wasn't getting her doctor or perfect pedigree to match me up with. Like I was some kind of overbred poodle.

Hudson was incredible, but he wasn't going to be steamrolled by her and he wasn't the type to tell her how perfect she was. He was too straightforward for that. He was successful, and I had no idea how much apartments ran or how much real estate cost, but I thought his apartment had been nice. The fact that he thought I was wonderful should have made her happy, but that wasn't anywhere on her checklist.

If I told her, she was going to demand to meet him. Was he even interested in doing something like that? Meeting families was supposed to be stressful when everyone involved was normal. My mother did not do anything "normal." Hudson was going to hate her.

From what he'd said about his family, they were nothing like mine. He'd talked about how loving his parents' relationship was and had all kinds of funny stories about them. All I'd been able to say was that mine worked hard and were too controlling.

Yup, he was going to hate her.

Weaving my way through the masses of students, I tried to turn my thoughts to something else, but it just wouldn't work. Hudson had said he was serious, but was that meet-the-parents kind of serious, or just the regular kind like he didn't want to date other people?

I probably should have asked.

I wasn't keeping him hidden and wasn't embarrassed by him, but I just wasn't sure he realized the can of worms I'd open if I said we were serious about one another. Dinner parties and expectations, nosy questions and judgments were enough to chase anyone off, and when you added my parents into the mix, it got even worse.

And how would I explain where we'd met?

Worms everywhere.

By the time I'd made it to the coffee shop, I hadn't figured anything out and had more questions than answers. Hudson must have been psychic, because by the time I'd finished ordering and was waiting for my drink, my phone was buzzing.

"Hi."

"Hello, Angel. Studying going well?"

I sighed, and he laughed. "No. I'm grabbing coffee and then I'm going to try again."

"Don't fall behind, because Sunday you're all mine, and I don't want to share you with books and flashcards."

"Sunday?" We hadn't really talked about plans for the weekend yet, but I was hoping I wouldn't have to wait that long to see him.

It was his turn to sigh. "I have a family barbecue on Saturday that I can't miss. I don't know how late it will run. Do you want me to call you after I'm free and see if you want to come over then? Waiting until Sunday isn't what I really want, but I didn't have a better plan."

"That's fine. I've got family stuff to do too." I felt stupid admitting how much I wanted to see him, but hiding it felt wrong. "I like the idea of staying with you on Saturday night."

I could hear the smile in his voice when he started talking again. "Me too. As long as you promise not to cook."

My face was probably blushing, but I laughed. "Your stove gets too hot. I've made scrambled eggs before. And bacon too. I really can cook. Besides, you were distracting me."

I could hear his grin in his voice. "I was reading the paper."

Snorting, I didn't try to hide my disbelief. "You were playing Angry Birds."

"I am far too old for children's games." He tried to sound snotty, and for a moment he sounded like he'd fit right in with my family.

"Then what about that candy game? I heard that song too before you muted your phone." My serious workaholic boyfriend had an obsession with the games on his phone. I didn't get the thrill, but I'd seen enough commercials and watched enough people play them in class to recognize the background music.

"I have no idea what you're talking about." He started off teasing, but then his voice turned more serious. "I was thinking."

That didn't sound very good.

"This weekend is going to be crazy, but would you be okay with having dinner with my parents next week? Something casual? I know it's early for that, but when she finds out I'm seeing someone, she's going to drive me nuts until I bring you over. Patience is not her strong suit." He was trying to keep it light, but I could hear the worry in his voice.

"You don't think it's too early…I mean…I'm not saying no, but…and I don't want to rush you…" And I was starting to sound like an idiot. Taking a deep breath, I grabbed my coffee from the barista and went to find a spot in the corner before I tried again, forcing the words out in one long breath. "My family isn't like yours and I'm going to have to tell them soon that I'm seeing you and you're going to hate them."

The relief was clear in his voice and made some of my stress fall away. "I'm not dating them. I'm serious about you. So it doesn't matter if they're obnoxious. My family, on the other hand, will drive you crazy by hovering and asking too many crazy questions."

"But you'll save me from having to answer them, right?" I was pretty sure that's what a boyfriend was supposed to do. Save you from their family. I just hoped I was up to the task.

"Absolutely. Unless it's my mother, then we'll both just hide. My dad is more laid-back." I could hear papers shuffling around in the background. He'd been working too much lately, but I wasn't going to fuss. He'd mentioned yesterday that they were starting to get some applications in to fill the other position, and I was keeping my fingers crossed they'd find someone.

"I know how to hide very well. I'll teach you." I'd perfected the art of disappearing at parties years ago. Find the right corner, and talking to strangers and pretending to fit in wasn't an issue.

"I'll hold you to that next time I piss her off." I could hear the relaxed smile in his voice. "You should have seen her when I told her I wanted to put off starting college for a year to work and take a break after high school. She went bananas. It wasn't safe to be around her for months."

"Did you take the year off?" I just couldn't picture him being that laid-back about life.

"Of course not, I'd just wanted to move out of the house and finally have some privacy. She'd been talking about me living at home the first year and getting used to college first. Hell, no, I wanted to explore all kinds of things, and living at home wasn't the plan. After I agreed to go to school, she didn't care where I was living as long as I went."

That never would have occurred to me. I was shocked. "I... you're devious."

He laughed. "And you love that about me."

He was right. It was also the first time he'd used that word. I tried to tease him back and not let him hear how much the word meant to me. "Of course."

I tried to think of anything to say besides the crazy things that were popping into my head. "You're going to have to teach me how to be more devious. Maybe then they'd railroad me less."

It might have come out whinier than I'd intended. I heard a squeak through the phone and I pictured Hudson stretching back in his chair, feet propped up on the desk. "You know, Angel, you don't have to go to get your master's if you don't want to. I think you'd be a good teacher, but if it's not what you want to do, then you should explore other things."

"Like what?" I sighed and sipped my coffee. "I don't have any other experience in anything. They didn't even let me apply for any of the teaching assistant positions that were open this year. I have nothing besides, well, you know, to put on a resume. I never even had a paper route or a lemonade stand."

I was kind of useless when it came to real-world skills.

"Hey, take a deep breath for me. You don't have to decide anything right now. I just wanted you to know that you had options." Hudson's voice was soothing, and I had to fight the urge to close my eyes and just soak him up.

"I just don't see any." People flitted in and out of the coffee shop, but they mostly ignored me. Panic attacks over majors and impending real life were too common to be interesting.

"We are going to find you some." I could almost hear the wheels turning in his head. "What do you like to do? What takes up your free time? I know you work a little and study a lot, but what else? Are you a secret crafter? Are you writing a manifesto to take over the world? Are you building the biggest Lego city ever in your dorm room?"

"Hudson." He made me smile and shake my head. "No, nothing like that. I don't have that much free time. Work is fun and doesn't take up much time, but I've got a list of people whose papers and essays I help edit for their English and history classes. It takes up a couple hours almost every day unless I'm careful and don't take too much on."

"Hey, that's something right there. I bet you make a good amount doing that."

"I don't really charge for it. Just enough on longer projects to cover expenses for stuff I don't want my parents to see."

He barked out a laugh. "They didn't even let you have your own bank account?"

"No." And that sounded sad, even to me. "I have a prepaid card I load with the money I earn. And Jake isn't even paying me. I wasn't willing to give him my social, so I'm only working for tips."

Hudson laughed so hard I thought he'd probably fall out of his chair. "The way those dirty old men talk, they should be tipping pretty good."

I made about a thousand a month working about once a week. I wasn't sure if that was good or not. I didn't have anyone I could ask because then I'd have to explain why. And the range of information when you looked it up online was overwhelming.

"I think so?" I wasn't doing it for the money and we both

knew it. Hudson just kept snickering, and I could tell he was trying to calm down, but it wasn't working.

When he finally caught his breath, he went back to the work conversation. Probably a good idea. "Have you thought about doing that? I know there are all kinds of companies and businesses who need editors. You could even start your own."

"Work for myself? Telling people how their sentences should be arranged?" I'd never thought of turning it into a job. English and grammar had come so easily that it had seemed mean not to help other people. When my own papers took a fraction of the time to write compared to other students, the very least I could do was help with reading over it.

"Why not? You might need a couple of classes to learn specific rules depending on what you want to do, but I don't think that would be a problem for you. My angel is brilliant." He had so much confidence in himself and in me, it was overwhelming.

"I…" With no idea what to say, I just nodded to myself and tried to organize my thoughts into something reasonable. It wasn't working. "I'll think about it."

"We'll talk about it this weekend and brainstorm some other ideas. Between the two of us, I'm sure we can come up with some other ideas. And at the very least, I'll learn more about what you like to do." The way he said it made me blush. The words weren't dirty, but something about the way he said it had me wanting to squirm.

"I'd like that." It was a weight being lifted off my shoulders.

Hudson would help. Maybe it was part of being a boyfriend or maybe it was the more take-charge dominant side of him, but either way I knew I wouldn't have to figure it out on my own. He didn't think I was pathetic or get frustrated that I had no idea what to do with my life. He just wanted to help.

I wasn't alone anymore.

15

HUDSON

"WHAT DO you mean he doesn't have a driver's license?" I was at my breaking point with filling the position, and I was ready to throw in the towel and hire someone from outside the area. I'd thought we'd finally found a great candidate. His paperwork had been missing a few things, but half the applications I'd seen were missing huge chunks of information, so I hadn't been worried.

When Jefferson Banks had applied, I'd thought we'd finally found someone for the job. He was taking night classes at one of the local colleges and had a good resume of administrative and office jobs that seemed to indicate he'd understand the regulatory side of things. He'd need training, but during his phone interview, he'd seemed like he would be a good fit with the company.

Wes gave me a look that was too measured and too careful. "It has not been necessary until recently. He said that he can have it in just a few weeks."

"Can we wait that long to get him certified? The last time I looked, he had to have a license in that job, not a CDL."

"That has not changed."

"There's something you're not telling me." I wouldn't say I was suspicious by nature, but I'd learned to be careful with Wes.

He didn't even try to hide it. "Yes."

"Lord. What is it? DUIs? Back child support? Jail?" He'd seemed like a decent guy in our phone call.

"No. Nothing illegal."

"Then what?"

"He is only seventeen and up until recently had not taken the required behind-the-wheel training."

Dear god, Wes was serious. "You're messing with me."

"No, I assure you, I am not."

I slumped back in the chair and closed my eyes. Fuck. My best candidate was barely old enough to drive. "We verified his references, right?"

"Of course." Wes was offended. "I checked with HR about that personally before the phone interview."

"Then what happened?"

"It's not on the application and never gets asked. His references checked out, and all had glowing things to say about him. We assumed he was on the younger side with the night classes, but we have several employees in that same location who are going to college through alternative means. The company pays for part of their tuition." Wes seemed like he was getting just as frustrated as I was.

I'd been at work late all week, and to be able to take off the weekend, I wasn't going to be leaving anytime soon. Working Saturday or Sunday wasn't an option, though. Neither my parents nor my boy were people I was willing to put off. Not being able to see Randall the last couple of days had been difficult enough.

"Is it even legal for him to take the job?" A few months ago, even a few weeks ago, I would have never even considered it.

Wes coughed. I wasn't sure if he was covering a laugh or

choking in shock. "Not without his license. He can, however, be a trainee in the position without his license."

Company policy had always been to hire someone local, as long as it was possible. In some of our international offices that could get interesting as well, but we'd never had a problem in that office before. Considering the low turnover we had, it had been several years since anyone there had been hired. And at that point, it was just a driver.

"He's really in college?"

"Yes." Wes's voice took on a more even tone. "He is a sophomore, and studying business just like it said on his application. What we could not find out on the initial paperwork was that he started taking college classes in high school and graduated early."

"There's no way we could have known." I took a deep breath. "He's the most qualified. He had to have started working when he was a child. Hell, he still is a kid."

"It seems that some of his initial jobs were for family members, and the age limit for obtaining employment did not apply." Wes did *not* like being surprised at work. We didn't even throw the guy a surprise party for his birthday. He wanted everything planned and laid out. This had to be making him crazy.

"I don't have the time to train someone for weeks, possibly months." I hated admitting that.

"Correct." Wes looked like he was ready to draw the line, even if I wasn't.

"Let me talk to Dad. Maybe he knows a way around the regulation or...or something." Maybe I could figure out a solution once I got some actual sleep. "I have to go over tonight and talk to them about the party. That damned barbecue is getting out of hand."

Barbecue should not mean having a catering company who came in and grilled steaks and hamburgers for five hundred rich people with more money than sense. "I still don't know why we just didn't have the fancy party they usually throw."

"According to your mother, who by the way has called twice in the last hour to make sure you'll be at her house tonight, she had to do something different to stand out from the crowd."

"Want to bet how many thousand-dollar cowboy hats there'll be at that party?"

"No." Wes gave me a look like he was done with my shenanigans. "And must I remind you that I am not your social secretary? Your mother is also demanding to know why you were not at brunch last weekend. You will have to explain that to her."

I groaned and my head dropped back against the chair again. "Crap."

The silence was deafening. I didn't even have to lift my head to see his disdain, I could almost smell it because the air was so thick with it. "Don't look at me like that. I am not hiding him. I talked with him yesterday about meeting them next week. I'm going to take everyone out to dinner and show him off. He's not being kept in the closet."

Wes gave a huff, and I knew he didn't believe me. "Can you imagine his initial impression if he meets them at this party? No, I don't think the money will be an issue, he doesn't have much sense with how much things really cost for some reason, but that is *not* how I want him to meet my parents for the first time."

I wanted to show him the nice, funny people who raised me fairly normally in spite of the money. Not the crazy woman who once a year played the millionaire's version of keeping up with the Joneses.

It seemed like I was finally getting through to Wes. "I can understand that."

"The crazy woman who keeps calling here is not the person I want him to meet." From what little I'd gathered about Randall's home life, his mother was insane and controlling, and

I wanted him to see that my parents were nothing like that. Right now, my mom could probably give *his* a run for her money.

"You *must* address that with her." His voice was stern, like a sharp, old-fashioned school teacher.

"Yes, you're not my social secretary." If the words came out dramatically and a bit sarcastic, it was because I'd heard them almost a dozen times this week.

"Do not miss another meal with them without calling her first." The firm tone of his voice said he wasn't going to negotiate with me on that point.

Ask him to work overtime and crazy hours. Fine.

Ask him to lie to my mother about where I was. No.

"I know. It was stupid." I grinned, and I knew it would drive Wes crazy. "It was worth it, though."

The coughing started again. I really needed to work on his sense of humor.

"I have the reports you asked for about the London expansion, and the numbers for last quarter. Once you have someone reliable in the local office, you will need to start scheduling additional trips abroad. The London office in particular."

"I know." We did our best to run the company like a family, and that meant lots of visits and support to the local managers who ran the offices. There were just only so many hours in the day. "I don't know how my father did it."

"Your father was not running a company this size." He *really* didn't like having the same conversation over and over.

"But—"

"*No.*" I got the schoolteacher tone again. "At some point, you will need to hire a vice president and more corporate staff. I admire your resolve to hire locally and keep the same family culture the business was founded on, but you are doing too much." There was a small pause, and his voice softened a bit. "Think of it as expanding the family. Not tearing it down."

"That's going to suck."

Wes sucked in a breath, and I had to grin. He was so easy to rile. "Hiring a manager is difficult enough. A vice president will make me crazy."

"The criteria necessary will narrow the selection down considerably, and we will not be able to hire strictly locally, but I do not foresee the same issues."

"As long as the right job posting gets listed."

"That was not a—"

"I'm not mad at anyone. I should have been more specific." Quite a few of our positions required a college degree. The local office here didn't because it would have made it almost impossible to fill the position. Once we'd realized that the requirements were wrong in the job details, it was easier to find applicants.

Easier but not easy. Big difference.

"Will you call my parents and let them know I won't make it for dinner, but that I'll be there for drinks after? I know it's not your—"

"Your father. I will *not* call your mother." Another line in the sand.

"Deal."

"I'M SORRY I'M LATE." I LEANED IN AND GAVE MY MOTHER A kiss on the cheek. "Everything ran behind today."

I got a disbelieving look, and she shook her finger at me. "That excuse no longer works. What is going on at work? You even missed lunch last weekend."

Shit.

"Everything is—"

"No. Your father is in the living room." It was like I was a teenager all over again. As I walked through the house, I remembered getting a similar greeting one time I'd come home late from a date.

I hadn't come out at that point, and they'd been convinced I was seducing some young girl. Instead, it had been an older guy who'd been seducing me. It'd been my first experience topping, and nothing they could have said that night would have made me regret it.

"That's fine. I could use a drink." Heading through the house, I tried to figure out what I was going to say. I needed... advice, but I wasn't sure how to explain it to him.

"You've had your mother worried." It wasn't much of a greeting, but I knew it was his way of saying that I'd made him worried as well.

I helped myself to a drink from the sideboard and went over to the couch. Settling in, I gave up trying to get it to make sense. "I told you about needing to get someone hired for the warehouse position?"

Dad nodded. "Yes, it's terrible about what happened to Albert."

I had to agree. "Patty says he's doing fine now that the stress of work is off him, but I'm struggling to find someone local to fill the position. It's been one thing after another. Now I've found the perfect candidate, but we've run into another problem."

Dad sighed. "It's been weeks. No wonder you've been overworked. I'd hoped it would get easier to find qualified people in that area, but over the years, it's gotten worse. Tell me about the new hire."

"Not hired yet. The snag is a good one."

Now I really had his attention. "What?"

I teased him with all the good parts first, college, the whole nine yards. "See, he's perfect."

"I agree. What's the problem, though?"

"He's seventeen. Doesn't even have a driver's license."

"*Wow.*"

Mom leaned forward, giving us both a long look. "But initiative like that has to be rewarded. You can't punish the young man because of his age."

"If we didn't hire him, it would be because of the license issue, not his age." I took a sip of my drink. "I'm just not sure what to do. The only option would be to hire him as an apprentice until he had his license, but I don't have anyone to train him or to step in and do the job for what could be months."

Just sharing the problem had me feeling lighter. I still wasn't sure what I was going to do about it, but knowing it wasn't just on my shoulders anymore made it seem less daunting.

Mom gave us a firm look. "I'm sure we can come up with something. Letting a young man like that go would be a crime."

I had to agree, but I wasn't sure how I was going to work it out.

16

RANDALL

"I'M NOT REALLY sure this is a good idea, Mother." I was really going to have to develop a backbone or start dragging Hudson everywhere with me. It was getting ridiculous.

"Of course it is. At your age, it's important to be seen with the right people. I'd be giving you the same advice if you were interested in women, so stop shaking your head. Dr. Richards is exactly the sort of husband you should be looking for. He comes from a good family, and that is very important when you start having children."

She'd realized I wasn't a girl, right?

"If I have kids, I'll probably adopt."

That was met with a scathing look. "Of course not. There are surrogates for that sort of thing."

Fuck.

I was going to be his stay-at-home little "wife," just one with a dick. Maybe I should get a T-shirt made that said "I've got a dick and like dick, so move on." Probably not helpful. And it wasn't like she'd let me wear it, anyway.

For today's "garden party where the caterers will be grilling steaks," I was wearing Mother-approved slacks and dress shirt that looked ridiculous at a barbecue, but evidently, just fine for that "garden party." Outdoor seating, grilled foods, bugs, yup, that was a barbecue. Not that she was willing to hear that.

Families as wealthy as the Merricks do not have barbecues.

Bullshit. I'd been to several of their parties, and they weren't as pretentious as everyone else. It would be just like them to have a barbecue complete with a country band and straw bales. Everyone there would just be in thousand-dollar outfits and carrying around champagne, talking about how "quaint" it was.

Mrs. Merrick was going to drive the other wives crazy trying to compete with a better theme for every party over the next couple of months. As we walked around the back of the gardens, I could see several panicked society wives looking around, taking mental notes. By the time the season was done, we were all going to be sitting on hay bales at these types of parties and eating five-hundred-dollar hot dogs.

I hadn't even made it to my usual hiding spot at the Merricks' estate when Mother had spotted me and started dragging me over to meet "the doctor." I'd had every intention of fessing up about seeing someone. There just hadn't been time or privacy.

She was going to lose it, and I didn't want to have the conversation in front of dozens of witnesses. "I need to talk to you first."

I got a firm shake of her head and a pointed look that clearly told me to behave and not ruin her plans. I'd seen that face often, right before I got dragged into something stupid that wasn't me at all. Like cotillion and a master's program so I could be a college professor.

Shit.

At this rate, I was going to end up married before I could tell her I was dating Hudson.

It really was too bad he couldn't get me knocked up. Then

he'd be forced to marry me. She didn't seem to realize I was a guy, so maybe it was doable?

"No, you don't understand." We dodged what would have been an awkward conversation with one of Mother's frenemies, and she just waved as we charged past. At a socially acceptable pace, of course. Mother didn't run. "I have to talk to you."

She would just walk fast and with purpose to try to marry her son off.

Lovely.

"There is nothing to say. I don't know why you're dragging your feet. I have found you a perfectly acceptable match. Do you know how hard that was? There are only a handful of gay men in our social circle, and even fewer that are socially acceptable. Unless I want to see you matched with degenerates, social climbers, or gigolos, he is your best option." The whispered words were said through a clenched smile. No one would possibly be able to tell that she was dripping with anger.

"But—"

"Dr. Richards, it's nice to see you here today. I'm so glad you could make it." She magically turned off her anger as a man came around a large bush that had been strategically placed to give some privacy to the back of the yard.

Great. She was arranging romantic rendezvous for me.

"Evelyn, I've told you to call me Jonathan." His smile was as fake as hers, but he wasn't ugly.

His dark hair was cropped close in that generic rich-guy way, and he looked like he went to the gym on a regular basis. The fact that he was honestly somewhere around my age was impressive. I'd been half-expecting some well-preserved fifty-year-old geezer.

"Jonathan." She fluttered like he was the most important person there. God, she was laying it on thick. "I'd like to introduce you to my son Randall. He's finishing up his master's degree before he gets his doctorate."

It felt like she was listing off my accomplishments, like they were some kind of awards you'd list at a dog show. Jonathan reached a hand out smoothly to shake mine. "I've heard a lot about you. Becoming a professor must be interesting."

Since when?

And how much had he heard about me?

Shaking his hand felt weird, like I was being sized up. I didn't care what he thought, but if he liked me it was going to be a problem. Mother would never forgive me for chasing off her doctor. I wondered for a moment if Hudson would let me sleep on his couch after she tried to kill me.

I probably couldn't go back to the dorms after that.

"It's nice to meet you." Short and boring. Hopefully, he'd get the hint or find me tedious and wander off.

I got a don't-you-ruin-my-plan look from Mother before she gave Jonathan another smile. "I have a few people I must say hello to. I'm sure you two would like to get to know each other better, so I'll just step away. We really must talk about the hospital soon, Jonathan."

Fuck.

"Of course, Evelyn, you have a wonderful insight into the fundraising side. I look forward to it." He honestly seemed sincere.

Shit.

As she walked away, I tried to figure out some way to hide or to force her to take me with her. Nothing. Jonathan turned that smile back toward me and took a half step closer. It wasn't inappropriate, but he was definitely trying to say something with the move.

I took a large step backward. It gave me more maneuvering room, but unfortunately, put me out of direct sight of the rest of the party. Not good.

"I understand you're a pediatrician." That should be boring and safe.

"Yes, neonatal. There's just something about seeing all those little babies that makes me want a family of my own." Another might-be-sincere smile broke out on his face.

Damn it.

I couldn't tell if he was serious or not, but red flags were going up everywhere. I was going to be married off before this fucking party was even over. I was definitely not going anywhere without Hudson ever again.

My brain liked that idea, and the mental wandering it wanted to do was downright dirty. Dragging it back to the issue at hand was hard. But necessary. Very necessary. "It's nice that you're ready for that step. It will be years before I can even think about something like that. My doctorate program, and then gaining tenure and all."

I was doing my best to tell him to back off, but it didn't seem to be working. I just got an understanding smile, and he stepped closer again. "I'm sure your plans would be flexible if you found the right man."

Shit.

He was too sure of himself and too confident that he knew exactly what I would agree to. What had she told him? "I'm going to have to step away and find a restroom. If you'll excuse me."

I ran.

Well, I walked very purposefully away from the perfect doctor who wanted a family and babies. Hell, I wasn't ready for all that. I wasn't even sure if I'd *ever* be ready for that. I hadn't even thought about it. Picturing a family with Jonathan-the-doctor was impossible, it made my skin crawl.

Now, picturing a family with Hudson was different. I wasn't any more ready for it, but I could see him with a baby or running after a kid learning to ride a bike. It was easy. It didn't mean I was ready to be sold off and bred like some kind of omega in a dirty romance novel.

It was time to hide.

I had another half hour before the food would be ready, and I couldn't decide if it was better to make a run for it now or later. A sit-down dinner would have meant I'd have to wait until everyone was mingling over drinks afterward or I'd be noticed, but with something like the barbecue, I had more options. I just needed to think.

The Merricks had several half-baths on the main floor. Two of them were easy to find, one off the main foyer that was tucked in a hallway for privacy and the other toward the kitchen for the staff. But they also had a small one that was awkwardly shaped and around a corner near Mr. Merrick's study.

In the past, it had probably been some kind of laundry room or even closet, but now it was a tiny bathroom that no one ever went in at their parties. I'd hidden there multiple times. It got a little warm in the winter, but overall, it wasn't a bad space to wait in.

Working my way through the crowd of people in the yard wasn't difficult. Everyone was trying to outdo each other, and I wasn't high enough on anyone's list to matter. By the time I reached the house and entered through the side door, I was feeling slightly relieved. Just a few more seconds and I would be free.

Well, safe in the bathroom.

It would have been harder to hide if everyone had been gathered in the house, but the nice weather meant that most people were outside, except for a few stragglers that were easy to dodge. The caterers in the kitchen didn't care who was in the house as long as I stayed out of their way, and other than some voices coming from the study, there was no one.

I quietly walked around the door to the study and breathed a sigh of relief when I got past it without being noticed. I was almost home free when I heard the voices in the study getting closer. As I finally made it into the bathroom, I felt the weight of everything start to move off my shoulders.

Leaning against the door, I pulled out my phone.

You might need to come rescue me.

No point in hiding the crazy from him if I was going to drag him into the mess next week, anyway.

What have you done, Angel?

Like this was all my fault. I sent back a little emoji with a halo.

Nothing…crazy woman has gone nuts and I need my knight in shining armor…she's trying to sell off the maiden to the highest bidder…

There was a cough in the hallway that sounded almost like a laugh, and I froze, afraid someone had found the bathroom. When it quieted and I could only hear whispers, I looked down at my phone.

I'd gotten a smiling emoji that seemed to be doubled over with laughter.

You're not a maiden anymore. But I'll come rescue you. It seems like I have to stake my claim before someone else steals the fair prince.

Thank god.

Where are you, Angel?

I was starting to feel guilty about taking him away from his family thing. Not a lot of guilt, because someone had to get me out of here, but still…

Can you leave now? I don't want your family to hate me.

I heard another chuckle from the hallway and tried to be as still as possible. Why were they still out there? Thankfully, Hudson's reply came back quickly.

I'm going to drag you over here. They'll love you. I just told them about you, so the timing is fine. This thing is boring and will go on for hours.

Another ton of bricks was lifted off my shoulders.

Thank you.

I got another smiling emoji with lots of teeth showing.

You're going to owe the handsome knight who is coming to rescue you.

I didn't mean to laugh, but one escaped anyway, and the voices out in the hall quieted for a moment. Shit.

Not wanting Hudson to think anything was wrong, I pushed aside my worries and texted him back.

Dirty, wicked things, huh?

A little devil popped up in response.

Of course. Now where are you so I can come start collecting on those dirty favors you owe me?

I was terrible at directions and had no idea of the address of their house. Shit.

It's probably the other side of town from you. It's a gated community with big houses. Mill Crest Estate.

I sent that part and tried to think of how to describe the house.

I'm sorry I don't know the address. It's a big Mediterranean house that's toward the back of the development. I'll meet you out front.

There was a long pause, then he responded.

Angel, do I tell the guard at the gate I'm with the Merrick party?

"What?" I texted back before I could process what he'd written.

Yes?

How had he known that?

Angel, are you hiding in the bathroom?

I looked around. I'd told him that I hid during parties, but…

Yes. How did you know?

The response was immediate.

Angel, open the bathroom door.

It was a weird instruction, and I didn't really want to leave, but…Straightening, trying to look like I hadn't been in the bathroom for an excessively long time, I opened the door.

"There's my angel." I heard the words, but it wasn't connecting.

"What?" My head popped around the half-open door.

"Come here." Hudson's deep, soothing voice chased the last of the nerves away.

"You're here." I was too excited to question him right away. I just threw myself against his body, loving the way his arms wrapped around me.

"Of course, I told you I had a family barbecue to go to."

Huh?

"Hudson Merrick?" I was starting to connect the dots.

He smiled and brought a hand up to caress my face. I gave in to the urge to close my eyes and just leaned against him. "I should have thought to ask your last name, Angel."

"Hamilton," I mumbled against his chest, not willing to move away from him for a second.

"Of course it is. Your mother is batshit crazy. Sorry, Angel."

I just laughed. "Yup, you do know my mother."

"Who is she trying to give my angel to?"

"Some boring doctor."

"Oh, the pediatric one?" He didn't seem surprised.

"Yes, he doesn't take hints well."

Hudson kissed my head, and I could hear the smile in his voice. "How about I keep the sexy pediatrician away from you?"

"Yes, please. He is hot, though." I giggled. "According to my mother, he's the only gay man in her circle who's not a degenerate. What did you do to be put on the wicked list?"

She should have thought Hudson Merrick was a great catch. I'd been avoiding people at parties for years, so it wasn't surprising that I hadn't met him before. "Wait. Your mother always calls you Matt."

He laughed. "Matthew is my middle name. She called me Matty for years, and when I wanted to start using Hudson, she had a hard time. She's doing better now, but it's taken a while."

"You don't look like a Matty to me."

Hudson snorted. "No, that's what I tried to explain to her. Mothers don't listen."

I cracked up laughing. "Oh, I know, and you never said why she thinks you belong on the naughty list."

Hudson shrugged and tightened his arms around me. "I've dated people exclusively in the scene for years. And that meant most of them weren't in the right social circle. About two years ago, I was seeing a guy seriously, and people were scandalized to find out he was a massage therapist."

That was it?

"Well, that got you on the naughty list, evidently."

"My parents didn't care, but it was the talk of the town for months." Hudson's hands started moving in slow circles on my back. "Your mother is going to have a cow."

"Yup." I nodded. She was going to lose her marbles. Not only was she not getting the doctor she wanted, I was dating the son of her rival who dated the help.

"My dad probably likes you." He'd admire Hudson's business instincts and drive. Now that I'd connected the dots, everything was falling into place.

"I get along great with him."

Probably better than I did.

"Well, this is why the cute little rabbit ran." Jonathan's voice rang out from the end of the hall.

Great. Just great.

17

HUDSON

I TIGHTENED my arms around Randall. I wasn't sure if I was claiming or protecting; maybe both. "He's taken, Richards. Go find someone else to seduce."

The guy got on my nerves.

There was nothing specific to point out and say, "Yes, that's why he's a douche," but there was something about him that made me want to punch him. So to keep my mother from killing me, I stayed away from the dick. Usually.

"His mother doesn't seem to think he's taken." Richards smirked, tempting me to reevaluate the idea of laying into him. "I've heard for weeks how sweet and perfect her son is."

"I'll say this one more time, even though I know you heard me. He's taken." He'd been away for several years with school and his residency, but I'd heard through the grapevine how he hadn't changed much. The rumors were still about seduction and then breaking things off, his MO since we were teenagers.

Before Richards could respond, footsteps echoed down the hall. The clip of heels on the hardwood said it was a woman, and I hoped it was mine coming to see what the drama was. If anyone could smooth this over and keep Randall's mother from losing her shit, it was her.

No such luck.

"What is going on here? Rand, this is not the kind of behavior that—Oh."

"Somebody just shoot me." The words were low, and I was probably the only one who heard Randall's dramatic whine, but I had to fight the urge to smile. I had a feeling she wouldn't find it funny.

"Rand! What are you doing?" Her voice was almost shrill, and I could see the anger building. Could she not connect the dots?

Randall took a deep breath and pulled away. I would have preferred keeping him close, but I was going to do my best not to egg the woman on. "Mother, I think you know my boyfriend, Hudson Merrick."

He took another slow breath and stood up even taller. "I tried to explain to you before you introduced me to Dr. Richards, but—"

"But nothing. This is ridiculous." She honestly seemed shocked. I wasn't that bad of a catch. "I introduce you to a perfect gentleman and you chose this...riffraff?"

So maybe I smiled at that one.

I ran a multi-million-dollar company. My parents both came from old money, and in *any* circles would be classified as well-off and nearly labeled socialites. I stood to inherit more money than I knew what to do with, and yet I was still in the same category as if Randall had been caught dating the maid, or butler in this case.

"It's nice to see you again, Evelyn." I tried to sound pleasant and appropriate. She just gave me a scathing look.

"What have you done to my son? Did you seduce him?"

She really didn't seem to get he wasn't a virginal young girl she got to auction off. Weird.

Randall sighed, not bothering to hide his growing frustration. "Mother, I'm an adult."

Evidently, just not in her eyes.

"Absolutely not. Look at the decisions you make when left on your own. Living in the dorms has corrupted you. And where did you meet *him*? I've done my best to introduce you to the right people and find you a proper match."

Richards was leaning against the wall, smirking. He was having a great time watching the drama unfold. He really must have been looking to settle down, because her clear hints at her vision of their future didn't make the douchebag doctor blink an eye.

Well, tough shit, because Angel was mine.

"I *have* found a proper match." Randall looked angry on my behalf. He might not stand up for himself, but it looked like he was more than willing to fight the monster for me. So cute. "He is smart and has done an incredible job of growing his business and thinks the world of me."

I leaned close and gave his head a kiss. "You're right. I do."

She looked at Randall like he was being ridiculous. "That is *not* what is important."

Since when?

"Mother, I am sorry you don't approve, but I am not leaving Hudson because you disapprove. I think it's time that I start making my own decisions." He took another deep breath and grabbed my hand, squeezing tight. Looking her right in the eye, he continued, "And I have other decisions that I will be making shortly about my education and potential career. I will let you know once I have everything planned out."

"You what?" Her voice echoed through the hall. "I've had that planned out for years. It is a very suitable career, since taking over your father's business is not a viable option."

"I have to find the right career for me, not something that is suitable to you." He said it softly, like he really wasn't sure why he had to point it out to her.

"If you think I'm going to pay for you to become some kind of…" Her voice trailed off. Evidently, she couldn't think of something terrible enough right away. "You've got to be kidding. I have invested time and money in your education. This is not acceptable."

She'd invested time?

And the money? His parents weren't quite worth what mine were, but she probably spent more on spa trips in a year than they did on his college education. She hadn't even been willing to send him off to an Ivy League school where she'd have to loosen the reins, so she couldn't complain.

"I'm sorry you feel that way." Randall was firm but much more polite than I would have been. I was barely controlling myself as it was. "That is not going to change how I feel. I think it's time I take more control over my life."

Her expression could have frozen us both to the spot. "We will discuss this when we get home. I expect to see you at the car immediately after the party." Then she turned and walked down the hall.

Richards laughed and straightened up from where he'd been relaxing against the wall. "Oh, I think I dodged a bullet on this one. Marrying into this family would have been *interesting*."

As he walked down the hallway, he called out a short, "Good luck," and smirked.

Randall sagged against me and cuddled close. "Do you think I could sleep on your couch for a day or two if she does something crazy like refusing to pay my dorm fees?"

"Oh, just ignore her. Although if Hudson doesn't think that's a good idea, you're more than welcome to stay here." Mom to the rescue. "I didn't want to intrude. I think my presence would have just made things worse, but I heard what Evelyn said, and you don't need to worry about a thing."

Randall stood up and tried to look presentable, straightening his clothes and giving my mom a fake smile. "Thank you for your kind offer, Mrs. Merrick. I'm sure that won't be necessary."

"You've always been so polite, Rand. But the offer is genuine if it comes down to that." She gave him a tender look, then started shaking her head. "I don't know who she's fooling with that money talk. You came into your trust at twenty-one just like Hudson did."

"What?" Randall seemed confused. "Trust?"

Mom gave him a long look. "They didn't tell you? I only know because we have the same investment advisor, and he made a comment one time about modeling your trust on the one we set up for Hudson."

Randall shrugged, still clearly lost. "I know there is some money set aside for me, but I think it's tied up until I turn thirty."

My mother waved her hand. "That's ridiculous. We can call the advisor if we need to, but I'm positive you've had that money for several years. Hasn't she been bringing you papers about it? Maybe something you need to sign every year?"

Randall nodded slowly. "Yes."

"It wouldn't surprise me if it were Power of Attorney paperwork. She's always been a little too controlling." Mom shook her head. "We'll get it all figured out. I'll have James give your father a call. I can't believe he'd be party to something like that."

Randall glanced down at the floor, then seemed to force himself to stand up straighter. "We don't talk much. So I wouldn't know if he was aware of what was happening or not."

She sighed and gave him a look that told me she was dying to hug him and make it all better, but she restrained herself. Barely. "You got the short end of the stick on parents, that's for sure. I'm very sorry, Rand."

"Thank you, ma'am."

"Oh," she waved her hand, "no company manners here. Call me Andria, please."

Randall gave her a hesitant nod. "Thank you, Andria."

She beamed at him and nodded. "Better. Now you two have your discussion, because it sounds like you clearly haven't been doing enough of that. Then I'll see you outside in a few minutes. Did you hear me, Hudson? Just a *few* minutes."

I got a stern look, like she knew I was going to get up to trouble, then she started walking down the hall. "Five minutes, boys."

Randall looked over and grinned. "She knows you really well."

"Too well." I laughed and pulled him against my chest. "I'm sorry your mother lost her marbles."

He sighed and wrapped his arms around me, tucking himself close. "It was bound to happen. I couldn't keep blindly following her. Thank you for helping me."

"Hey, you did everything. You'd even started making the decision to stand up to her before I came along. The job? That was your first act of rebellion." I had to smile. As far as rebellious acts went, his could have been much worse. She should have felt lucky. I'd driven my parents crazy.

"It was? I hadn't really thought of it that way." He lifted his head and gave me a kiss. "Will you help me figure out if I actually have money?" Then he frowned and shook his head. "That sounds pathetic."

"No, it sounds like someone who hasn't been given much freedom." It was a bit like he'd only been able to see the real world from a window and was now getting to explore it for himself. "You are not alone, Angel. No matter what, I'm here."

"You don't think I'm stupid for not questioning things sooner?" His brows pulled together, and I could see the worry in his eyes.

"No, absolutely not. You wanted to make her happy. She's your mother." Just not a very good one. "And you are more than welcome to my couch, my bed, and anything else you need, Angel."

I pulled him close again and gave him a tender kiss. Letting it slowly deepen, I finally pulled away when we were both breathless and hard. "Time's almost up, and she will come find me, just so you know."

Randall giggled and grinned. "She's *nothing* like my mother."

Thank god for that.

"Come on, before we get distracted." I gave him another kiss, quick and innocent.

He smiled and took my hand, stepping back. "Can you give me a drive to the dorms later? I came with my parents, and they were going to take me back after, but all of a sudden that doesn't seem like such a good idea."

I barked out a laugh. "Probably not. I would love to take you to the dorms, Angel. Or you can come to the condo with me?"

Randall squeezed my hand. "Yes, that sounds perfect."

"Do you need anything from the dorms? Books?" I wasn't sure if he'd gotten everything done or not.

He shook his head as we rounded the corner to head back toward the living room. "No, I got everything done earlier."

"Wonderful. Then we have the rest of the weekend to ourselves."

He stopped as we got to the living room. "What about work? You still haven't hired anyone, have you?"

I grinned. "I've got it all figured out. You're going to love it. I'll tell you when we get home."

"You look like the cat that ate the canary. What did you do?" He knew me too well, too.

"Nothing terrible. It's perfect. And it wasn't completely my idea; Dad helped." Randall smiled, and I knew he was pleased that I'd talked about the problem with my parents. "See, I'm not that stubborn."

He was still smiling as we got to the back door. I saw him take another deep breath, and he looked around subtly. "You're not going to leave me alone, right?"

"I will never leave you alone, Angel." The words came out filled with more emotion than I'd intended.

"Thank you, Hudson." Then he looked around and, seeing that we were alone, kissed me quickly. "And thank you, Master."

My wicked angel.

18

RANDALL

I WAS USUALLY BORED after those parties because I'd been hiding in obscure places like bathrooms for extended periods. Going back to Hudson's place, everything felt different. I was tired, but it was deep inside, like I wanted to curl up and continue to hide from everything.

His hand reached out and started caressing my neck. I closed my eyes and soaked up his warmth. "You look exhausted, Angel."

"It's not that late, though, and all I did was make small talk." I shouldn't have been this worn out.

"And then there was everything with your mother and my mother and everyone learning about us dating." I had a feeling his list could have kept going, but mercifully, he stopped. "I think you had a longer day than you realize."

Possibly.

"I'm fine."

He might have laughed, because he made a strangled sound, then started to cough. *Dramatically.* "It wasn't supposed to be funny."

"Then don't say ridiculous things with such a straight face."

His hand tightened around my neck and something about the small change had my muscles relaxing and almost sinking into the seat.

"That feels good." I was fighting off the urge to yawn.

"You just relax and let me make you feel good. We're almost home and then we'll take it easy tonight." His voice was soothing, and I loved the fact that he wasn't going to make me decide anything.

"Okay." I was good with whatever he wanted, as long as I didn't have to think.

The ride to the condo didn't take long. I probably should have realized he lived in a nicer part of town, but I'm not sure I would have connected the dots and guessed who he was even if I had. "Should I have realized you were a Merrick, or at least part of that crowd?"

I was starting to think I'd been stupid, or at the very least, a little naïve.

"Not necessarily. I don't think I ever said my last name, and money never really came up. It wasn't that important to either of us." His hand kept caressing my neck and shoulder, so I pushed the worries away.

"I wasn't hiding it from you." His voice seemed stressed, so I opened my eyes and turned to look at him.

I wasn't sure what he meant. "Of course not."

He'd taken me to his house. He'd talked about work. I just hadn't understood what they'd meant. "Do you think I was?"

Was that what he was worried about?

Hudson smiled. "No, Angel, I just didn't want you to think I hadn't said anything deliberately."

"Oh, okay." My brain was going in too many directions to process his fears. All I knew was that he really understood that my parents were crazy, and he still liked me anyway. He'd said I could stay with him if the batshit crazy woman got me kicked out of the dorms.

"Do you think she'll actually do it?" Okay, so it was a leap in conversation topics, but Hudson followed perfectly.

His face darkened, but I could tell he was trying to hide it from me. "She can't get you kicked out of school, because more than likely, she's already paid tuition for the year. And you got in on merit, not because of who your parents are. Dorm fees might be different, but you don't like living there, anyway."

He had a valid point. "But—"

His finger touched my lips. "I wasn't done." He grinned for a moment before his features evened out, and he kept talking. "Worst-case scenario, you have to find someplace else to live. My mother wouldn't have mentioned your trust unless she was sure. Monday morning, we're going to make that our top priority. I use the same guy, so we'll go in and talk to him. Once that's squared away, you'll have plenty of money to find an apartment or just pay the dorm fees, if that's what you want."

He was making it sound simple. But she'd been so angry.

"I can see your mind turning in circles, Angel. So what if there's no money? You work more hours at the bar. You really don't understand how good your tips are, Angel. That right there would pay for most of your living expenses and a chunk of your tuition. If you were inclined to let me help, I wouldn't mind at all. But if that made you uncomfortable, then I'd help you get student loans or figure out another job." He said it like it was so easy. Just a simple problem with lots of different ways to fix it.

"You're sure it's not going to be more complicated?"

"I'll be with you every step of the way. And if I don't know the answer, we have my parents. They already love you. I could see it in my mother's face." His hand squeezed my neck again, and he went back to focusing on the road.

It took me a moment to realize we were parking behind his condo and not on the street where the taxi had dropped me off. There were a few spaces tucked at the back of what looked to be a nice garden. He turned off the car and leaned over to give me a tender, almost innocent kiss. "My tired angel."

I just nodded. He was right. I was his, and I was tired.

He moved away to climb out of the car and walked around to my side. Going all the way to the condo seemed incredibly difficult, so I wasn't in a rush. I'd managed to unbuckle my seat belt by the time he opened the door, but that was about it.

"Come on, Angel. I know exactly what we're going to do."

Part of me was hoping it would involve ice cream, but I didn't say anything. I'd already had a steak and a delicious chocolate mousse. I wasn't that hungry. It just sounded good.

Hudson took my hand and helped me out of the car. Wrapping his arms around me, he let me rest against his chest, and I just breathed in his scent. "I know you are overwhelmed right now and everything feels like it's weighing down on you, but I promise we will get this worked out. And once she sees that you aren't going to do what she wants, she's going to back off and let you make your own decisions. I know it."

I wasn't as confident as he was, but I didn't want to worry anymore. "Can we pretend everything is fine? Just for tonight? I don't want to talk about her anymore."

I just wanted it to be Hudson and me…Master and me was an interesting idea too.

"Absolutely. We're going to relax, and it's going to be just the two of us."

"Perfect." I gave him a tight hug, then straightened. "I can function. Let's go."

"I never had any doubts." He grinned and took my hand.

As he led me through the back yard, I had to marvel at the little garden. It was almost like an old English garden with flowers everywhere and a winding path. Not the formal ones, but the cottagey styles that made you want to sit and relax.

"This is beautiful."

Hudson nodded. "There's a guy on the first floor who's

made the garden his project. Evidently, no one else in the building was interested in the space, so he got permission to set it up. I think it's great. It's what sold me on the property."

It probably would have sold me too. It was quiet and relaxing. "It's incredible."

"Yeah, he's some kind of banker or something, and I think uses it as a way to relax. You see him out here a lot in the evenings and on the weekend." Hudson opened the door and stood back to let me walk in.

As we got to his place, I was feeling more like myself. Less exhausted and more numb, probably. But I'd take it. His condo was dark, but he didn't bother turning on all the lights, just one lamp as he led me through to the bedroom.

I wasn't sure what the plan was, and I wasn't going to ask, but I was still surprised when he led me into the bathroom. When I'd been picturing the possibilities, the bathroom hadn't really been on the list. Still, I simply waited and held his hand. That was all I wanted, anyway, just to be with him.

He turned on the lights and gave me another tender kiss before letting go of me. Hudson stepped toward the tub and turned on the water. The bathroom was starkly white, but in a magazine kind of way. My brain hadn't really been working the last time I'd seen it, so I'd never really analyzed it. It wasn't boring or ugly, it just wasn't what I pictured from him.

"Did you design the bathroom?"

He laughed. "No, it was already renovated. It's kind of cold looking, but I love the tub."

Hudson leaned down to plug the tub, then came back over to me. "We're going to get you a bath. Then we'll see if we want to watch a movie or just cuddle in bed for a while."

I just nodded. "Okay."

He gave me an understanding smile and another kiss before he started stripping off my clothes. Not having to decide what to do or worry about what he wanted was perfect. I knew my opinion would matter if I actually had one, but he seemed to understand when I needed him to take control.

As he stripped off the layers of clothing, he sprinkled kisses along my body and let his fingers caress and tease. By the time I was naked, he had me shivering and hard. His hands wandered over my body as he led me toward the tub. When I was about to step in, I looked back at him. "But you're getting in too, right?"

He smiled. "If that's what you want."

"Yes." Oh yes, I wanted him naked with me, not just watching. He could watch next time.

He had his clothes stripped off before I could even get my hands to work enough to help. Eventually, we'd have to do stuff like this when my brain was working from the start so I could touch and explore him too. So far he'd kept me so turned on, all I'd been able to do was follow his lead. I had a feeling it would be a while before that changed.

Hudson stepped into the water and sat down, then helped me to sit in front of him. Hudson chuckled as I cuddled into his chest. The water was so warm it made my skin tingle. It was perfect.

"I'm glad my tub is big enough for both of us. I don't use it that often, and most of the time, it seems like a waste of space."

I had to agree. "It's huge compared to the rest of the apartment."

His tub was almost the same size as his kitchen. Okay, well not that big, but definitely not in proportion with the rest of the house.

"Having you here like this, I'm starting to think a big tub is a necessity." His words were low and sent sparks through me. I could almost hear the dirty things flashing through his mind.

"Oh, yes…" I lost track of what I was going to say as Hudson started trailing his fingers up and down my chest. My cock bobbed in the water, begging for attention, but Hudson just kept tracing circles around my nipples until they were tightly pebbled and I wanted his touch so badly I was shaking.

Begging crossed my mind, but I wasn't sure if that would get me what I wanted or not.

Finally, I broke. "Please!"

He gave a dirty chuckle, but finally brushed his fingers across my nipples. "Does my dirty angel want something? I thought you were tired."

So had I. But curling up had a different meaning in my mind now than it had in the car. "I need you…please…Master…"

"Does my little slut want his master's touch? Does he want to be teased and taken?"

The naughty words were everything I needed to hear. "Yes! Please!"

I wanted to forget everything, and I knew he could give that to me. I wanted to be the center of his world and know how much I meant to him.

The words would come eventually for us, but the actions were what was most important. I'd heard the words from my parents, but *I love you* didn't mean much when the actions said you weren't that special. Hudson showed me in every little way how important I was to him.

"Well, if that's what my naughty angel wants." One hand moved down to take my cock in a rough grip. "But remember, who controls this cock?"

So. Fuckin'. Hot.

"You do, Master." Someday I would just combust saying that.

"Good boy. Then you remember the rule about coming."

It wasn't really a question, but I felt the need to answer him anyway. "I can't…can't orgasm until you give me permission."

God, that was hot.

"That's right." He started handling my cock like it was some kind of tool he was tossing around in his hands. Like it was his, and he could do anything he wanted with it. The desperate need to please him was the only thing that kept me from coming. "This is all mine, isn't it?"

He scraped a nail over the head of my dick, and I almost flew out of the tub. "Yes!"

I got another wicked laugh from him, and I knew more of the beautiful pain was going to come eventually. He must have decided I was too close, because his hand left my cock and went back to teasing my nipples.

He'd run his fingers around the edges, then just as I was starting to fall apart and beg, he'd pinch one or flick it with his finger. Hudson rolled them in his fingertips, sending fireworks through me. I'd always known they were sensitive, but I'd never played with them as roughly as he did. They would ache tomorrow, but that would just make everything hotter.

I loved carrying the memory around with me. It was a physical reminder that everything wasn't just in my head.

Absentmindedly flicking the tips, he started talking again, the dirty words making it impossible to think. "I think we should get these pierced. We can go tomorrow. I've been doing some research, and I found a place that's highly recommended."

His almost businesslike voice as he was talking about what he wanted to do to me just made it even more erotic. "We'll start off with something small, but once they're healed, we can get you something flashy that will show under your shirt at work."

He was serious?

It wasn't the first time he'd brought them up, but...piercings?

"You want to...and...in my..." He started tugging on them, pinching them just hard enough to make my cock jerk in the water and making it impossible to think.

"Oh, yes. I know you've thought about it. I can see it in your face when I talk about it. You want these pretty tits pierced, don't you?" The wicked words kept flowing out of him, deep and sexy. "You want me to show you off and play with them while your cock gets harder and you're so turned on you nearly explode."

I shouldn't agree with him…it was just…naughty. "But I can't…that's…"

"Wicked?"

"Dirty?"

"Bad?"

"But…" I wasn't sure if I was supposed to agree with him or not, but it was all those things. That didn't keep me from wanting it, though.

"But I want these sexy little things decorated, and it's going to make them even more sensitive. I'll make you writhe and beg, and they're going to feel incredible rubbing against your shirt." He tugged them so they were sticking out from my body. "And I could put little weights on them. You'd love how that felt, my little pain slut."

He pinched them so hard I cried out, and my hips start thrusting up out of the water, desperate for more. I couldn't deny what the pain did for me. I was his little pain slut, and he loved it. There was no reason to fight it.

"Please, Master…Please!"

"Does my little slut want more?" He laughed again as I nodded and begged. "What does my dirty angel need?"

"You, please…fuck me…I need…" I needed him inside me. Making me fly with that perfect feeling of being possessed and wanted…loved.

"If that's what my boy wants." One hand reached down to start tormenting my cock. I was going to come if he pushed me much further. It was all too much.

"Please! I'm going to…you have to…" The feel of his fingers rolling my nuts in his hand chased the thoughts from my head.

"Into the bedroom then, I'm going to stretch you out and—"

"No! Now please! Don't make me wait." I was shaking, and

my cock was so hard it ached. All I needed was one good thrust of his dick, and I knew he'd send me flying. I couldn't wait, and walking would be impossible. I needed to come.

"The condoms are in the bedroom, Angel."

"I'm clean! Was a virgin! Just fuck me, please!" I might have been just a little out of my mind. But it was his fault, so I wasn't going to feel bad about it.

"I'm negative, Angel, I was tested, but I don't want to rush you into that." His hands started trying to soothe me, but calming down wasn't what I wanted. "I can show you my—"

He loved me, and he wouldn't do anything to put me in danger. I knew that with every fiber of my being. "Make love to me, Master."

If he said he was safe, he was safe.

Hudson paused for a moment, then his hand started moving roughly on my dick again. Yes! "Does my boy want to be filled with his master's cum?"

Was it stupid to admit I hadn't thought of that part?

"I...and you'll...I..." My brain was definitely broken.

My mind was looped on the endless, naughty things I'd seen online, and I couldn't move past it. Imagining Hudson doing all those things to me was incredible.

"I think that's a yes." He moved his head, and his teeth scraped along my neck, making it even more difficult to function. "One day, I'll fill you full of my cum and plug you before your shift. How does that sound? Do you want to be my cum slut?"

His lightning fast reflexes were the only thing that kept me from orgasming. Just as my cock started to throb, he grabbed the base of my dick tightly. "Naughty boy. Do you have permission to come yet?"

"I'm sorry." It was breathy and filled with desperation. "I couldn't help it."

"Very bad boy. I'm going to have to punish you later." The

words should have sounded terrible, but the thread of excitement in his voice made me want to moan.

"But I didn't come." I wanted the punishment, but I didn't want him to think I was bad. I knew it didn't make sense, but I was too far gone to think it through.

"You were so close though, my wicked angel." His tongue traced along my ear. "I have to make sure you remember who controls this sexy cock."

"You, Master." I wasn't ever going to forget that.

"Reach out and grab the lube, Angel." The words took a minute to work their way through my brain.

Lube?

Eventually it clicked, and I saw the container at the edge of the tub. He didn't move his hands away, so it was slightly awkward, but relief poured through me when I finally gave it to him. Crazy images were flashing through my mind and it was all I could do not to beg. I ached.

"That's my good slut." The words were naughty and beautiful. "Turn around and straddle my legs."

Moving was harder than it should have been. My legs were like rubber, and my cock was so hard I was afraid even the brush of the water would make me explode. By the time I'd moved to kneel over his legs, his cock was slick and ready, bobbing out of the water.

Hudson's hand reached between my thighs to tease my hole. "One day I'm going to have you show me how you work this little hole, how you stretch it and fuck yourself. But I don't have that kind of patience today."

One finger sank deep into me, making my toes curl and a low moan escape. It wasn't anywhere near enough, but it was so good. He fucked me slowly while I knelt over him, begging and shaking. When I started humping back on his hand, he spanked my ass. The pain spread through me, dragging out a low groan.

"Naughty boy." He pulled almost all the way out of me, then

sank back in with two fingers, so he couldn't have been that mad.

"I need you...Hudson, please..." Two fingers quickly became three. Then his patience must have run out, because soon, I was empty and needy as he guided me over his dick.

"Remember the rule, Angel." He growled out the words, passion and need etched in his face.

"I'll—" Whatever I was going to say was lost. I eased down and took him deep in one long motion, and it chased every thought out of my head.

The water wrapping itself around me made everything even better. It was like fingers continually caressing every part of me as his dick stretched me wide. Hudson moaned, and his hands gripped my hips so tight I could feel his fingers pressing into my skin.

"Move, Angel, ride my cock, Boy." It wasn't until he growled the command out that I realized I was just grinding on him in slow circles.

There was no reason to wait. I wanted that stretch and the incredible feeling of his cock taking me. It took a few minutes to figure out the rhythm, but in the end, it was just like breathing, a perfect in and out that happened without even thinking.

"God, so beautiful. My angel. I could watch you forever." One hand moved to wrap around my cock, and he gave it two long, slow strokes before it all became too much.

"Hudson!"

He tightened his grip on my dick and shoved his hips up, slamming his cock into me. Fire shot through me. I exploded. He felt even bigger as I clenched around him and my orgasm crashed over me. I could hear myself crying out, but I couldn't hold anything back. Wave after wave of pleasure kept coming as he fucked into me, his hips working frantically.

When he finally came, the feel of his cum shooting deep inside me had me shaking with pleasure and emotion. It was the ultimate proof I was his. When we were both finally done, I collapsed onto him, water sloshing in the tub. His cock started to soften, and his arms wrapped around me.

"My sweet, dirty Angel." The loving words wove their way through me, and I felt tears prickle at the back of my eyes. I'd finally found someone who understood all of me and only loved me more because of the things that made me awkward and different.

He made me feel like his beautiful, dirty angel.

EPILOGUE

HUDSON

EVERYTHING HAD CHANGED SO MUCH in one week. Sometimes I turned around, expecting our lives to still be just like they were only a week before, but nothing would ever be the same again.

"Why won't you tell me where we're going?" The laughter and pure curiosity in Randall's voice made me smile.

"Because then it wouldn't be a surprise." And I wanted to see the disbelief and shocked arousal flash on his face when he realized where we were going.

He laughed and cocked his head, wiggling in the seat. "What kind of surprise needs something like *this*?"

I reached over and gave his hard, trapped cock a pat. "The best kind."

The week had been so stressful for Randall that I'd wanted to give him something as a reward, a surprise he'd remember forever instead of holding onto the memories of meetings and hard decisions. I reached out and turned on the radio, giving my blindfolded lover something to focus on.

He'd done his best to push away the disappointment and frustration of Saturday and relax the rest of the weekend, but I knew it had been eating away at him. I'd even put off the trip to get his nipples pierced to give him more time to process everything. Monday morning, he'd sat in silence as I'd called my broker's office and arranged for a meeting.

I hadn't been shocked at the outcome, but I'd been hoping for something different for Randall's sake. He'd come into a huge inheritance at twenty-one, and evidently, some of the paperwork he'd signed was a Power of Attorney, giving his mother control of the funds.

She'd managed it well, and the money had grown under her guidance, but James had been shocked to discover that Randall knew nothing about the money or the investments. He'd made it very clear that when he'd talked to Evelyn, she'd said Randall had understood everything.

There had been a few tense moments where he was clearly concerned about legal problems, but once we'd explained that Randall just wanted answers and access to the money, everything went much smoother. We'd talked to James for hours about the different investments and how much income could be safely pulled from the trust without eating into the principal, and had gone over things so Randall knew exactly what he had. I never wanted him to feel helpless or trapped by someone else's decisions again.

Giving control to someone else should be a choice, not something that was stolen from him.

His head had been reeling, but in the end, he'd arranged for money to buy a car and made sure there would be cash available if he needed to pay tuition. Randall said he was going to continue his master's programs until he knew what he wanted to do, but he'd also started looking at some advanced editing classes as well, so I knew that idea was still rolling around in his head. I just kept telling him he had plenty of time to make decisions, and I would be there for him every step of the way.

"Tell me about their first day working together?" He gave me a pout, clearly looking for attention.

I reached into my pocket and gave the remote a long pulse. He arched back in the seat and moaned, pleasure making him gasp and thrust his hard cock into the air. "I think I said it went well."

When he could breathe, he shook his head and slumped back in the seat. "But...but we got distracted before you could tell me details."

"I honestly wasn't sure how it would work, but it went better than I could have expected." When my mother had suggested a solution, I'd thought she'd lost her mind. She was going to remind me forever not to question her logic.

I just think she wanted to get my father out of the house.

"But your dad seems to like it? It's not weird that he's technically working for you?" Randall grinned and cocked his head, turning toward me like a puppy.

"It's going to get weird, eventually. Is it terrible that I'm waiting for him to screw up? Just something small, like forgetting to send in the reports or something." I had to sigh. I was a terrible son. "He's probably going to do a great job."

"Don't sound so sad about that." Randall was almost giggling.

"There's no learning curve for him in that job. When I was learning the different jobs in the company, it felt like there was a mountain of information. This is too easy for him."

"Well, he has to teach the other guy how to do it. That might be hard."

I sighed dramatically. "No, because he's smart and on the ball too. It's going to go great." It really was working out well. The new guy was grateful for the opportunity and very willing to learn, and it got my dad out from under my mother's feet. It was good for everyone.

I buzzed the plug just to watch him squirm again as I was

pulling into the parking lot. I'd had to pull a few strings, and it was costing an arm and a leg, but it was going to be worth it.

"Sit tight. I'm going to come around and help you out of the car." Leaning over, I gave him a peck on the cheek and quickly got out.

He was finally starting to relax as I opened the door and reached out to take his hand. He frowned and turned his blindfolded head from side to side. "Where are we?"

"Do you really think I'm going to tell you now? Just when we're getting to the good part?" He had to have heard the laughter in my voice because he gave me an exaggerated pout. "Nope, that's not going to work."

I pulled him close and wrapped my arms around him. Giving him a long, slow kiss, I let my hands wander down his back to nudge the plug I'd slid in right before we'd left. It was flush to his body, but that wasn't going to matter where we were going. It wouldn't have mattered even if I'd put in the vibrating one with the long base.

He reached up to cup my face as I pulled back. "But I look okay? I mean, no one will…notice?"

"That you're hard and have a cock ring on? Or that you have a plug in and are ready to be bent over and fucked?"

He flushed, and his hips thrust forward to grind his cock against mine. "Both…either…"

"Both, eventually, but I promise you won't care in just a few minutes." As soon as he figured out where we were going, he was going to be too surprised to care.

"You love making me nuts."

"Of course." Moving to stand beside him, I wrapped one arm around his waist and grabbed one of his hands. "It's not that far to the door. I'll tell you when you need to step up."

"We're going inside somewhere?"

"Yes, but that's all I'm telling you."

I got another pout, but he carefully walked with me, paying

attention when I told him about the step and as we walked through the door. As we headed into the building, I could hear bass thumping from the speakers.

"Where are we?" His voice was quiet, and I knew he was straining to hear any clues.

We were quickly greeted by a large gentleman that looked like a Wall Street broker in a nice suit and tie. "Mr. Merrick, welcome. I think we have everything arranged to your satisfaction, and we're glad we could be of service."

"I appreciate your help and discretion." He'd been very accommodating and open to my out-of-the-ordinary request.

"Discretion? Hudson, what did you do?" Then Randall seemed to remember we had company, because he cleared his throat. "Um, thank you for having us."

The owner smiled, clearly taken with Randall already. "You're very welcome, sir." Then he pointed down the hallway. "Right this way."

We followed him through the building, Randall straining to hear and muttering under his breath. As we finally came to the end of the hallway, I stopped and nodded to the owner. He walked off, giving us a moment of privacy.

"Are you ready to find out what we're doing?"

Randall was vibrating with excitement, but he was starting to get cautious again, so I gave the remote a tap. "Hudson!"

"Yes, Angel?"

His voice dropped down to a whisper. "You can't do that. I hear other people here."

"They don't care. I promise."

"But…" His brain was working overtime. But not for long.

"Do you want to know?"

"Yes." It was a bit hesitant, but he squeezed my hand. "You're making me crazy."

I laughed and palmed his ass. "Because you look so sexy when you're nuts. Now, are you ready?"

"Yes." His reply was more confident that time.

"Here we go." Releasing his hand, I reached up and carefully removed his blindfold.

"Where—" His eyes opened, and his mouth dropped open.

"I'm sure you can guess where we are." If the mirrors, poles, and half-naked men didn't clue him in, he was more innocent than I'd thought.

The G-string-wearing men on the other end of the room waved and smiled. Randall awkwardly waved back, too polite to ignore them. "Hudson!"

Laughing, I pulled him close again. "They're going to give you lessons, and one day I'm going to have Jake close down the bar for the night and you're going to do a private show for all the regulars who love to watch my angel."

"Hudson." He looked back and forth from me to the strippers. I think I broke him.

"I'm going to watch my angel strip down and have so much fun." His eyes were too wide and his breathing too fast for it to be fear. Yes, he was nervous, but he also wanted it. Badly. "They're going to show you how to take off your clothes and show off that sexy hard cock you've got."

"Hudson!" Yup, broken.

Knowing he'd do better once he was actually doing and not thinking, I gave his ass another pat. "Go on. Show me. You want to do it for me, don't you?"

He wanted it too, but I knew being able to put it on me made it easier, so I was willing to play along. Nodding, he looked back and forth again.

"But, Hudson…" The words came out breathy and filled with emotion.

"Go on, show your master how sexy you are." I leaned in and gave him a kiss.

He blinked up at me, then peeked over at the strippers

again. "They do this for a living." It was very matter-of-fact. His own confidence boost.

"That's right. So they don't think it's shocking at all. And they're going to be so surprised at how good you do, because my angel is incredible. Go show them how sexy you are." He gave my hand a squeeze and let it go.

One step turned into two, then he paused. Was it too much?

Randall turned back to me, a shy, emotional smile on his face. "Thank you, Hudson."

"You're welcome, Angel."

"I love you, Hudson. This is the best surprise ever." The words cracked a little, and I could see how hard it was to hold everything inside.

"I love you too, Angel." Smiling, I pointed to the guys. "Now go show them how wicked my angel can be."

He gave me another smile, then took a deep breath and started walking again. My sexy, nervous boy walked across the room, head held high and a sassy swing in his walk. He was so cute and so perfect. He would keep me on my toes, but I knew there was no one else I wanted in my life.

He was my sweet, dirty angel. My perfect angel.

ABOUT MA INNES

M.A. Innes is the pseudonym for best-selling author Shaw Montgomery. While Shaw writes femdom and m/m erotic romance. M.A. Innes is the side of Shaw that wants to write about topics that are more taboo. If you liked the book, please leave a short review. It is greatly appreciated.

Do you want to join the newsletter? Help with character names and get free sneak peeks at what's coming up? Just click on the link.

https://www.subscribepage.com/n1i5u1

You can also get information on upcoming books and ideas on Shaw's website.

www.authorshawmontgomery.com

ALSO BY M.A. INNES

His Little Man, Book 1

His Little Man, Book 2

His Little Man, Book 3

His Little Man, Book 4

Curious Beginnings

Secrets In The Dark

Too Close To Love

Too Close To Hide

Flawed Perfection

His Missing Pieces

My Perfect Fit

Our Perfect Puzzle

Their Perfect Future

Beautiful Shame: Nick & Kyle, Book 1

Leashes, Ball Gags, and Daddies: A M/m Holiday Taboo Collection

Silent Strength

Quiet Strength

Beautiful Shame: Randall & Hudson, Book 2

Too Close To Break (Coming March 2018)

AVAILABLE ON AUDIOBOOK

Secrets In The Dark
  Flawed Perfection
  Silent Strength (Coming Spring 2018)
  Quiet Strength (Coming Spring 2018)

ALSO BY SHAW MONTGOMERY

AVAILABLE ON AUDIOBOOK

Bound & Controlled Book 1: Garrett's story

Bound & Controlled Book 2: Brent's story

Bound & Controlled Book 3: Grant's story (Coming March 2018)

Bound & Controlled Book 4: Bryce's story (Coming April 2018)

Bound & Controlled: The Complete Series (Coming May 2018)

UNTITLED

Do you want a peek at what's coming up?

The Accidental Master, Coming April 2018

JACKSON

"Melissa! What the hell did you put in that Facebook ad? I'm getting all kinds of crazy-ass responses!" Storming into the house, I slammed the door behind me. She was dead meat. She had to have pulled that shit on purpose.

What the hell had I done to her?

I headed for her bedroom, stomping up the stairs. Knowing my sister, she was probably buried up to her neck in books and papers. Normally, I wouldn't let myself into her house—I actually had manners unlike some people I could name—but this time, she'd gone too far. She wasn't going to be able to hide from me.

"Melissa!"

"What?" She was sitting on the bed surrounded by papers and notebooks, a half-eaten sandwich hanging off a plate. "What crawled up your ass and died?"

"What—" She wasn't serious? "I'll tell you what *'crawled up my ass'*—because it's your fault. I want to know what you did to my business. That ad you set up? The one you said was a simple Facebook ad that would help my business? What did you put in it?"

I tried to take a deep breath and slow down, but I was too angry and too confused. "I'm getting all kinds of crazy people calling me, and the emails are even worse. I had one from a guy in some weird European country I've never heard of, who wanted to know if I did training packages and not just individual sessions. He said he couldn't figure out from the site what kind of training I did with my pups. He wasn't talking about *dogs*!"

"Huh?" She seemed lost. "What do you mean he wasn't…"

Her voice trailed off, and she got a faraway look in her eyes before they widened, and her mouth opened. "*Ohhh…*"

"Do you know how long it took me to figure out he wasn't referring to beagles or boxers? Entirely too *fuckin'* long!" Just the fact that it'd taken almost five minutes before I finally understood what he was talking about had been the most embarrassing thing. I was a to-each-his-own kind of guy, but it was getting ridiculous.

"Oh, Jackie, I'm—"

I broke in. "Don't you '*Oh, Jackie*' me. I'm not six years old following you around like a lost puppy—ha! Puppy! What did you do?"

"Jackson, I'm so sorry. It was an accident—" If I hadn't known her so well, the innocent, crushed look would have worked.

"Like the *accident* where you dumped water on my pants at dinner? Or the *accident* where you put salt in my tea?"

"No, this was a *real* accident, and come on, I wouldn't do something like that to you. You know me."

Bullshit. "The salt incident was last month, and you dumped the water on me last week when you thought I was rude to the waiter."

"You *were* rude." She looked like she was still ready to take up the fight for the lazy waiter.

"That's not the point. *What did you do to my business?*" My voice was getting louder, but I couldn't control it. She'd talked me into trying some new marketing ideas, and now it looked like my business was falling down around me.

She slumped down onto the bed and gave me her best innocent look. If she'd pulled it on anyone else, they might have believed her. "I haven't fallen for that in years, so cut the crap."

Sighing, she slouched back against the pillows. "It *was* an accident. I promise. I was putting it together late the other night, and I must have mixed some things up. I'll go in and cancel the ad and get it corrected."

"Bullshit. You *accidentally* changed my dog training business to some kind of kink training center?" We might have tortured each other a bit over the years; it was what siblings did after all, but this crossed the line.

Dragging a pillow over her head, she moaned. This time her frustration sounded real. "I can't believe this."

"*You* can't believe it? What about *me*? I'm the one having to answer emails with naked pictures in them. Well, mostly naked. Several had tails!" They were insane and weird and a little too…no, I wasn't going down that rabbit hole right now.

I'd worry about my sanity and my new porn preferences another time. "*Just tails*, Melissa!"

And erections…

And teasing, happy smiles…

And I had to get back on track.

"I'm sorry! I'll fix it." She was still buried under the pillow, trying to pretend to be the injured party.

"How about I go into your work and say crazy shit about you? Let's see how you like that. You went too far with the crazy this time!"

"It wasn't on purpose!"

Yeah, she accidentally turned my dog training center into a

BDSM business. At least, I thought it fell under BDSM. Maybe not? "Bullshit! How can you even think I'd believe that line of crap?"

"Because it's true. I got the copy mixed up. I was putting up another ad at the same time!"

I was finally starting to connect the dots. Maybe. "What? What kind of ad were you posting?"

Had I stepped in something personal? Melissa had always been more private than I was about who she dated, but I didn't think she'd leave out something—who was I kidding? She would never have said anything. "Mellie, I won't tell Mom if that's what you're—"

"No, it's not for me. I'm not that interesting." She sighed again and looked up at the ceiling like she was praying for patience or for God to strike her dead. "I'm a writer. My newest book just came out, and I was putting together a Facebook ad that was designed to target specific people. I mixed them up. It was late, and I must have attached the wrong pictures."

She did what?

"You're a writer?" By the look on her face and the people who'd been emailing me, she didn't write historical romance. "You write dirty books? Does Mom know?"

"Of course she doesn't. No one in the family does. I really didn't mean to mess this up for you. I'll fix it right now. It's not hard to cancel the ad, and I'll do my best to help clean things up online. I'm sorry, Jackie."

"Stop it with the nicknames. You're just trying to manipulate me."

"Ja—"

"No. You're not going to distract me."

"I'm sorry, Jackson. Just don't say anything about the books. Please? I'm not ready to answer the questions." She finally looked like she wasn't trying to give me a line of shit.

"Yeah, there'd be questions, all right. Puppies? What do you write? Do I even want to know?" Probably not.

She huffed and gave me a stern look. "I write love stories that are a little unique."

"That's an understatement." At least, judging by the emails I was getting.

"Not helping, Jackson." She was starting to get her back up, and I could see that in her mind, she was building it up so that *she* was the injured party.

I shrugged. I wasn't trying to help; I was well past that. "I just want to know that you can fix this without damaging my business. And don't give me that look. I'm the one whose company is going to explode. Do you know what will happen if this gets out?"

Half of my clients were little old ladies and their uncontrollable yappy dogs. They wouldn't find it funny. Hell, I wasn't finding it funny. I'd been shocked when I first figured out what was going on, but after that, I'd been…confused. So confused, I'd spent several hours looking things up online before I'd come over to scream at her.

"I know." She sounded like a put-out teenager again.

"Just fix it. And no more advertising online." Everything was fine. I shouldn't have let her talk me into it to begin with. Training classes were always full, and I'd always found word-of-mouth referrals to be the best way to build up my business.

"But it's a great way—"

"No."

"Fine. But you're not going to tell Mom, right?"

"My telling Mom is the least of your worries. You should be thinking about how I'm going to get even with you!" My revenge was going to be good. It was just going to take some time to pick out exactly how to get her back.

"That's not fair! It was an accident."

"That's what you said about the salt *and* the water. I'm not falling for that bullshit again." I really should learn to watch my back around her better.

She got that innocent, sweet look again. "I'm your sister. That means you should trust me."

"Hell, no. I may love you, but most of the time, I don't believe a single word out of your mouth." The writing thing was starting to make sense.

I got a grin from her. "Aww, you say the sweetest things, Jackie. I love you too."

Deciding to ignore the nickname, I shook my head. "That's all you got out of that sentence?"

She gave me a smile that looked half-psychotic and half-sweet. My family was nuts. "I focused on the important part. Now, go away. I have work to do and an ad to take down."

"You really write dirty books? Like for a living?" I was still having a hard time wrapping my mind around it.

"Yup, and I'm doing pretty well." She smirked like she was very proud of herself. And probably glad she had someone to brag to now.

"Like *quit your day job* kind of good?" How much could you really make writing dirty books?

"None of your business." Then she gave me a teasing grin. "But possibly."

I shook my head and started for the door. I didn't want to know any more. If I wasn't careful, she would tell me exactly what she wrote just to make me crazy. "You're going to fix it right now? Like take the ads down and no more interesting people emailing me?"

"I'll fix it."

"You'd better." I wasn't sure what I would do if it kept up. It was getting to be too much.

Pulling into my driveway, I threw the car into park and slouched back in the seat. *God, what a long day.* Maybe I could have found more humor in the situation if it wasn't so confusing. I'd come out young, and while I wasn't a man-whore, I dated a lot and assumed I knew myself.

I was starting to suspect that I didn't understand myself as well as I'd thought.

Once I'd figured out what was going on, I'd checked my email and had seen about a dozen, all with the same theme. They might have said they were looking for training, but they'd just been guys in desperate need of attention and someone who understood. The emails had been from a variety of places. There had even been one older guy who, as he put it, "was finally ready to figure out who he was."

I'd replied as politely as I could. Partly because I was raised with manners and was representing my business—but a bigger part was because I felt bad. It was crazy, but I felt terrible that I couldn't help them. Completely nuts, but I hated telling them it was a mix-up.

The notification sound on my phone made me sit up and function. Swiping my finger across the screen, Melissa's text came up.

Sorry…ad taken down…shouldn't have any more calls.

Texting back a quick acknowledgment, I forced myself to get out of the car. Heading inside through the kitchen, I grabbed a beer out of the fridge and went to the living room. I had tons of budgeting and paperwork I should have been doing, but my brain wasn't going to cooperate so I walked back to my bedroom.

I could still see the pictures in my head every time I closed my eyes. And not just the ones that had been emailed to me. The videos and photos I'd seen online had been mind-blowing. I'd seen my fair share of porn, but I'd always gone more mainstream when I looked for something to watch.

I'd never even been curious enough to explore any of the fetish sites that were out there. Maybe I was boring, but I was pretty content with watching a blowjob scene or two guys going at it. The most adventurous thing I could remember looking at was a threesome video that had been pretty hot. But *nothing* like what I'd seen earlier.

It was so much more erotic than I'd expected.

There'd mostly been amateur stuff, but that made it even better. They were real people who found it arousing, not just actors getting paid. To say I was conflicted would've been an understatement.

Setting my beer down on the nightstand, I grabbed my laptop and took a deep breath. There couldn't be *that* many more emails, because the last of the phone calls had been before I'd gone over to Melissa's. Pulling up my account, I lay down on the bed and logged in.

There were only a few, and most of them were actual clients. In fact, there was only one that I didn't recognize, and the email address gave it away immediately: *twofunnypups*. Hating that I was going to have to burst someone else's fantasy, I clicked on it.

To Whom It May Concern:

We just wanted to thank you for training pups. So much of the BDSM community is focused on other things, and it's hard to find opportunities like this. My friend Cooper and I are pups. We've been friends for a long time and we have fun together, but we've always talked about taking things further. Training sounds interesting, but we have some questions.

First was if you would take pups to train together. We don't do playtime apart. We're not exactly a traditional couple, but we've always been in this together, and I don't think I could

do it without him. The second was if you helped single pups find an owner or master? Cooper and I have looked online, but it's hard because most masters want just one pup. Two seems kind of a handful. And I won't lie. We are. We try to be good, but things get out of hand. Cooper's easily excited and playful, and I don't know how I would describe me.

The ad didn't say how much training costs, and it was kind of vague about if we would have to live there. I think we're close to you, so that might not be a problem, but we both have jobs that we can't afford to lose. We're not sure how it would work. So I guess we have lots of questions, not just a couple. But even if you can't train two pups like us, we wanted to say thanks. Seeing the ad made us feel good—like there were other people out there like us.

Thank you,
    Sawyer

My heart sank.

It was sweet, and the picture they'd attached was just as cute. And thankfully, a lot more clothed than some of the other ones had been. They were sitting on a bench, arms slung around each other, grinning for the camera. They looked young but luckily not like jailbait.

I hit the reply button and looked at the email for a long time. It shouldn't have been hard. I'd written the reply so many times already; it felt like I could've done it in my sleep. Looking at the picture, though, I tried to guess who was Cooper and who was Sawyer.

They wanted to belong to the same master.

What did Sawyer mean when he said they weren't exactly a couple?

Telling myself it didn't matter and it wasn't my business, I took a drink of my beer before I set it down and started to type. It was going to be a long night. Knowing I needed to respond, no matter how hard it was going to be, I began.

Dear Sawyer and Cooper,

Printed in Great Britain
by Amazon

39542074R00131